A COMPLICATED JOURNEY

Steve Dressing

#6

**Number 6 Publishing LLC
Virginia**

2019 Number 6 Publishing Paperback Edition

This book is a work of fiction. Names, characters, businesses, places, and incidents are either used in a fictitious manner or entirely imagined creations of the author. Any resemblance between the fictional characters and actual persons, living or dead, is purely coincidental.

Biographical note © 2019 by Steve Dressing

Cover © 2019 by Nicola Goodwin

A Complicated Journey. Copyright © 2019 by Steve Dressing. All rights reserved. Printed in the United States. No part of this book may be used or reproduced in any manner whatsoever without written permission except in the case of brief quotations embodied in critical articles and reviews. For information address Number 6 Publishing, 1799 Rampart Drive, Alexandria, Virginia 22308.

Science consultant: Dr. Courtney Dressing, Astrophysicist

Number 6 logo is a registered trademark of Number 6 Publishing LLC

Library of Congress Control Number: 2018915295

Dressing, Steve. A Complicated Journey.

ISBN 978-1-7321116-3-9

Keywords: Young – Adult – Fiction, Science Fiction, Space, STEM, STEAM, Astronomy, Rockets

1 2 3 4 5 6 7 8 9 10

Number 6 Publishing website address: number6publishing.com

A COMPLICATED JOURNEY

TO THOSE WITH MINDS OPEN TO THE POSSIBILITY THAT WE ARE NOT ALONE IN THE UNIVERSE, AND TO THOSE WHO DREAM OF ACHIEVING GREAT THINGS, REGARDLESS OF THE CHALLENGES THEY MAY FACE

Acknowledgments

Special thanks to my wife, Julie, who continues to support my writing endeavors, and to my adult children for their ongoing encouragement. Courtney inspired me with her academic achievements and her work detecting and characterizing planetary systems orbiting nearby stars. She also reviewed the book and has graciously allowed me the freedom to stretch the science a bit. Kelsey provided valuable help with the design layout, while James has supported Number 6 Publishing in many ways through his new business adventure, Klik Media LLC.

In addition, my young reader friends Anthony, Shaan, and Saira provided very helpful reviews before publication. I am grateful for and extend a special thank you to Lee Ann Hennig for her review and support. Finally, thanks to those who have directed, designed, and championed our efforts to explore and study space over the years. You have opened our eyes and minds in ways that are immeasurable.

PART I

1

BROWN DWARF

"For those of you looking for a second home, do we have a real estate deal for you!"

Vera frowned as she listened to the news anchor dumb down her recent discovery of potentially habitable planets within our Solar System. "Real estate? Really?" she called out to the group of Finder Mission peers huddling with her to watch the newscast. They were reporting on major findings from the annual gathering of international experts in astronomy, astrophysics, and planetary science.

"Yes, Dr. Vera Daniels of Northern Science Academy announced today the likely discovery of three planets that may harbor life around a brown dwarf at the edge of our Solar System. Just a short commute away!"

⚜ ⚜ ⚜

"Fantastic!" Colleen Freeman cried out, watching the newscast from her living room. "Did you hear that Mom?"

"What, dear?" Mrs. Freeman asked from outside on the deck where she was grilling dinner.

"They found some new planets near Earth!" Colleen said. "We can go there some day."

"That's wonderful," Mrs. Freeman replied. "Get me a ticket." She knew little and cared even less about science. Colleen was the exception in her family; both parents were in business. Mrs. Freeman only cared about the things science could create for her, with absolutely no interest in how science did its job. Finding planets seemed to have nothing to offer her, so she ignored it altogether.

"Yeah, funny Mom," Colleen said. Colleen had only basic knowledge about brown dwarfs, stars that failed to ignite and give off light. She did know, however, that they could have planets orbiting them, were hard to find, and were typically smaller than the Sun, details she could discuss only with the few in her high school astronomy class who had similar knowledge. Actually, nobody in her class was at her level because Colleen was a child genius. Her classmates were generally six to eight years older than she was, a gap that made it very difficult for her to socialize with any of them. While they were suffering through acne problems and middle school weight gain, she was still working on double knots for her shoes. Now that her acne and weight problems had appeared, they were driving cars and going on dates. The only things they shared were their school classes and college options. When they needed answers to difficult questions or problems, however, they always came to Colleen.

Colleen was quite unrefined socially, partly because her brain didn't have room for that sort of thing, and partly because she had little opportunity for socializing. Kids her age thought she was weird, and the older kids didn't want to spend time with such a young kid. Her parents did little to find solutions to this problem, instead yielding to the temptation to just take care of themselves and let her deal with it. Shouldn't she be able to handle socializing if she was such a genius, even if she was just twelve? Her parents were clueless.

When classmates asked her questions, Colleen would usually give the answer and ask why they were too stupid to figure it out themselves. She had no compassion for them and could not begin to understand why they found things to be so much more challenging than she did. Colleen knew that she was smarter than they were, but she felt that they should be equally capable because they were in the same class. She often called them lazy, something that did not go over well. Many times, she was threatened with being stuffed into a backpack or being driven into the woods and left behind. Not that this would actually happen, however, due to the strictly enforced disciplinary rules at her school, but her classmates still lashed out because they found her frustrating and arrogant. Colleen never reported what they said, because she thought it was stupid and totally unrealistic. Although small, she was much too large for a backpack.

———

"Well, all of what we've done has once again been reduced to a tag line and a thirty-second story," Dr. Daniels lamented.

"At least it came up before the story about the runaway hog at the Iowa state fair," Carla Lòpez joked. Carla was a friend and planetary scientist at Hawthorn Tech.

Dr. Daniels rolled her eyes and chuckled. They all knew that their story would not be of interest to many people, but they expected it to be treated seriously by the press. All of those in the room remembered reading about the days long ago when science was disregarded and rejected by the masses because the country's leaders didn't want to believe the stories it told, particularly the story about climate change. Those days were just a memory now, but scientists still feared a return to those dark ages, and every slight was considered a step in that direction.

Although people once again respected science, its face had changed dramatically with females now dominating the fields. Young boys generally avoided science and math in school, instead focusing on business and the arts. This was a total change from decades earlier when females were aggressively recruited into math, science, and engineering careers.

Colleen was no exception to this trend, but she was unique because she was so gifted. About eighty percent of her classmates in science and math classes were females or non-binaries. Most boys just took the required math and science classes and then filled out their schedules with classes they preferred. Even when it came to science-fiction books and movies, boys showed little interest. Colleen, however, didn't notice this imbalance because she was too focused on her own interests.

"Can I sign up for this summer's national science program, Mom?" Colleen had wanted to go for years, but her parents thought she was too young to be away for so long. Their simple reasoning had nothing to do with her ability to thrive in the program, just that she was younger than they were when they first spent time away from home. Money wasn't an issue either because both parents had well-paying jobs.

"Are you sure you want to be away all summer?" Mrs. Freeman asked.

"That's nothing compared to when I'll be exploring planets as an astronaut." Colleen dreamed of seeing other worlds firsthand. "I'd love to go!"

"Perhaps you're old enough now," Mrs. Freeman said. "I'll talk with your father tonight and we'll let you know. When do you need to apply?"

Colleen provided all of the details about the

program from memory: application dates, fees, departure and return dates, locations where the program was hosted, packing guidelines, lodging options, etc. Everything.

"Northern, right?" Mrs. Freeman asked, using the nickname for Northern Science Academy.

"Yep, that's the closest, and I really want to work with Dr. Daniels."

"Who's she?" Mrs. Freeman asked. These days it was assumed that the scientist was female, a reality that Albert Einstein and friends would find unimaginable.

"She's the one who was just on the news. She found the new planets. She's a rock star," said Colleen.

"Oh," Mrs. Freeman said. She was a huge fan of rock-and-roll music from around the turn of the 21st century. "Like Bruce Springsteen?"

"Who?"

"Bruce, remember him?"

"What?"

"Oh, forget it," Mrs. Freeman said, not wanting to go down that path for two reasons: Colleen didn't care about music, and it would make her seem older than she was because Bruce had been dead for decades.

"Thanks, Mom," Colleen said, both for dropping the music discussion and for agreeing to consider letting her apply to the program.

With the week-long meeting coming to an end, Finder Mission team members were gathering their belongings and bidding each other farewell. There would be other conferences during the year, but this was the largest and the best opportunity to make and renew connections.

"Well, I need to get some sleep so I can catch my flight back to Northern," Vera said.

"I'm taking the tube," Carla said, referring to the magnetic train tube that linked the convention site to downtown Boston where Hawthorn was located.

"That thing doesn't bother you?" Vera asked.

"No, I've gotten used to the extra G force."

"What is it now, 3 G?"

"No, it's only 2 G. We're not astronauts!" Years ago, astronauts on the Space Shuttle were subjected to about three times the force of gravity, or 3 G, during launches. Safety standards for passengers on the magnetic train allowed a maximum of 2 G, and all riders needed to pass physicals before they were given the right to ride the train.

"That's still too much for me," Vera said. "Safe travels."

"Same to you."

2

BUSINESS

"I can go? Really?"

"Yes, Colleen, your father and I agreed that you can apply for the summer science program," Mrs. Freeman replied. "You still need to be accepted, so don't just assume you'll get to go."

"I understand," Colleen said, not in the least concerned that she would be rejected.

"Why don't you fill out what you can on the application form, and then ask me to help you with the rest," her mother suggested. Although not yet a teenager, she figured Colleen could handle that task as well as she could.

Colleen snapped her fingers and quickly accessed a holographic display of the application form. She vocalized answers to nearly all of the questions before swiping the display over to her mother in an adjacent room. Mrs. Freeman called out the remaining information and provided biometric identification to release funds to pay for the application.

"Thank you for your application. We will let you know if you have been accepted to the program within two weeks."

"Thanks again, Mom," Colleen said after hearing the automated confirmation message.

Colleen went up to her bedroom and spent the next several hours researching and studying several topics of interest to her, including the newly-found brown dwarf and its three planets. She was particularly interested in finding out if there was any likelihood that intelligent life could be found on those planets.

After many decades of exploration in space, humans still had not found any large lifeforms beyond Earth. Missions to Jupiter's moon Europa and Saturn's moon Enceladus had resulted in the discovery of primitive microorganisms but nothing with more than a few cells, let alone a creature as large as a fairyfly, the smallest insect on Earth. There were many discoveries of water and atmospheres on distant exoplanets, but these planets could not be reached by human spacecraft for closer examination. Humans had traveled to

Mars and established small colonies both there and on Earth's moon, but life was not found in either location.

Communication with intelligent life elsewhere in the universe had remained within the realm of science fiction. Wars among the stars could still only be imagined, and strange creatures with huge brains and telepathic powers lived only in the written word. The discovery of life on Europa and Enceladus generated great excitement, but the fervor died down as many could not grasp the significance of what was a huge step in the long journey to find other intelligent life in the vastness of space.

Colleen, of course, understood how important it was to find life, any life, beyond Earth. She knew that it meant that scientists were right about organisms existing elsewhere in the universe. It also kept alive the hope of finding more advanced lifeforms. This possibility, the chance that intelligent life could be found in space, is what excited her most about science.

Colleen was so driven by her interest in life on other planets that she failed to fully appreciate those living creatures who shared her space every day right here on Earth. While she would say she loved her parents if asked, she mostly just saw them as necessary parts for her growth and evolution. To her, they were more like a saw or hammer, tools needed to build a house, or a bat and ball needed to play baseball. They weren't to become part of the home or participate in the game but were simply needed to ensure that the house could be built or the game could be played.

This didn't mean that she treated her parents poorly. In fact, she behaved very much like other kids her age. She appeared to care about her parents enough, but not too much. Her parents were quite distant themselves, so they were perhaps the most unlikely people to notice anything unusual in their relationship with Colleen. All in all, they seemed to have a mutually beneficial, if not extremely unusual, relationship.

Tulip, the family dog, barked outside of Colleen's room, a sure sign she needed to go out back to do her business. She was a quiet dog, except when her bladder was full or she felt threatened, neither of which was a rare occurrence.

"OK, Tuly, hold on," Colleen said as she got up to take care of the dog. She hated the name "Tulip," but she was just two years old when her parents decided they needed a pet. Colleen had no say in choosing the name.

The Freemans believed they needed to have a child as part of their overall business plan. They didn't really have a vision for life, but they did map out the various elements of their lives that would be important to achieving their business goals. They believed without evidence that most successful business people had children, so they decided to have a kid, just one. Two kids would probably place too much strain on their careers. Dogs typically accompanied children, and it was best to ensure that the dog was gone when the child left for college. Because of advances in breeding and care options for pets over the past several decades, dogs now had an average life expectancy of about sixteen years. So, having the dog when Colleen was two would guarantee that it was gone when Colleen no longer needed their daily attention. They would then be free to spend all of their time on their careers, with the added benefit of being able to boast that they had done the "kid and dog" thing and were therefore fully credentialed business people.

They had no idea, however, that raising a puppy

while tending to a two-year-old would wreak havoc on their lives. Tulip was not easily house trained and neither was Colleen. Between the two of them, their daycare employee, Kate Troutman, was cleaning up messes five or six times each day. In addition, the constant yapping of the puppy and Colleen's frequent crying created such tension that Kate had reached out to a therapist for counseling on ways to cope. The Freemans, meanwhile, escaped the house as early as possible each morning and stayed late at work as a matter of routine until Colleen had mastered potty time and Tulip had learned the primary purpose of the back yard.

Colleen didn't remember anything from those early years, and she saw Tuly as simply another necessary part of her own development. She took the dog out to the back yard, cleaned up after her, and played around a bit before returning inside. This was a largely mechanical routine to Colleen, but Tuly appreciated it nonetheless.

3

ROGUE

Vera spread out on her desk printed versions of the eleven summer science program applications that had made it through Northern's screening process. She enjoyed working with young students during the summer as long as they didn't take too much of her time. The fresh faces and personalities renewed her energy, much like the arrival each year of a new class of college students. Reviewing the applications, however, was not something she enjoyed.

Within minutes she was able to eliminate all but three of the applicants. Budget constraints meant that she'd only have one student this summer. That would be a great opportunity for the student to have one-on-one time with the professor, but it also meant that the student would have no companion in the program. Vera did not want to spend a lot of time entertaining a high school kid, so, despite feeling a bit guilty about it, she assigned that task to her graduate students.

Vera called Jamie and Min to her office to have them help her finalize her choice for the summer program. Jamie was a strong student, while Min was struggling with his studies. Vera accepted him into the PhD program to increase the number of male students, but he didn't seem to have what it takes to survive, let alone achieve the highest degree possible in the sciences.

"OK, I've narrowed the list to three applicants, but we get to choose only one for the program," Vera said. "The applications are pretty short, so let's just go through them together and make our choice."

"I like this Colleen kid," Jamie said after a few minutes for review. "She must be a genius."

"But that's the easy pick," Min countered. "These other two have good grades and are several years older. I think they'd do better on campus."

"Don't worry, Min," Jamie kidded. "You'll be able to hold your own with a genius."

Min didn't laugh. He knew he was considered a lightweight in the program, and he had grown tired of hearing about it.

"Well, I agree with Jamie," Vera said. "Having a child genius would be an interesting experience. We could also sway her toward Northern later if things go well."

Colleen's lack of social skills was not something any of them could know about based on the application. They would experience that side of her in a few weeks when she arrived on campus.

Just as her students got up to leave, Vera received a message on her wrist phone. It was Dr. Lòpez.

"Hey, stick around," she said, "Carla says she has an important message."

As Jamie and Min sat back down, Vera cast the holographic image so all could see Dr. Lòpez.

"Hi, guys," Carla said. "Have you heard the news from Dave?"

"No, what?" Vera asked. They all knew that Carla was referring to Dr. Dave Davids, Carla's colleague from Hawthorn. Davids was a rising star in the field with several important discoveries already under his belt, including numerous brown dwarfs.

"He announced discovery of a rogue planet."

"Ah, another one of those buggers," Vera replied.

Rogue planets floated in orbits around the center of the galaxy instead of around a single star like in our Solar System. Some are huge gaseous giants, while most are dense planets more like Earth.

"Not just another one," Carla said. "This one is coming near us and may cause some problems."

"Whoa! How quickly? How close?"

"Here, look at this," Carla said as she transmitted a graphic showing the expected trajectory of the planet. "There is still a lot of guesswork, but it looks like it could have a significant influence on the orbits of our outer planets."

"Which, in turn, would have an impact on Earth's orbit," Vera said, fully aware of the delicate balance among planetary orbits in the Solar System.

"Yes, that's right," Carla said.

"So, we're in jeopardy of a doomsday?" Min asked.

"Let's not get ahead of ourselves," Vera cautioned. "But, yes, it's possible that the Earth could be torn apart, moved closer to or farther away from the Sun, or both."

"It all depends on how big it is and where it goes," Carla said. "I've gotta go now. Dave is pulling us all into this so we can gather more data and do some calculations. You can expect that you and others from around the world will be involved as well."

"Yeah, I'll bet," Vera said. "We'll do our background work so we're ready to help."

4

NORTHERN SCIENCE ACADEMY

Colleen snapped her fingers to see the message from Northern. She didn't celebrate her acceptance into the program because it was what she expected. Her mind raced, however, as she thought of the many opportunities at Northern and how she should use her time to get the most from the experience. Others might write a list, but Colleen didn't need to because she could remember every detail later.

Discovery of the rogue planet had filtered rapidly through the public conscience since the announcement a week earlier. While the exact path and timeline weren't yet fully understood, there was enough information available to create a wide range of reactions. Many saw it as an act of one god or another, offering various reasons for the threat and even more ways to ensure that the planet changed course to save Earth. Skeptics were also plentiful, and these individuals and groups provided numerous lines of "evidence" that the whole thing was a hoax. Some called for worldwide parties so all could enjoy themselves before the end. There were also many people who simply didn't care. A large number of people, however, had a much more measured response. They knew it would be over twenty years before the planet neared the Solar System, and they also knew from the reporting that there was no threat of a direct hit, just a question of whether it would come close enough to cause any significant impacts at all. They would wait and see what the details were and what the options were for saving Earth if necessary.

Colleen read as much as she could about the rogue planet discovery, while also continuing to dig for information on the brown dwarf and its planets. It was wonderful, she thought, that these two exciting discoveries came so close to the summer program. There was now a real possibility that she would be given important scientific work to do while at Northern because they would need all of the help they could find.

As another unchallenging year at school wrapped up, Colleen prepared for her adventure at Northern. Her parents left all of the details to her, rationalizing that if she couldn't plan for the trip then she wasn't ready to take it. In actuality, they were just too focused on themselves and their work to give it much energy. Colleen didn't mind, however, because she was up to the task, including planning for all clothing and supplies, arranging travel to and from Northern, and estimating how much it would cost. Lodging and meals were handled by the program, and Colleen wasn't the type of person who needed a large slush fund for nights out or off-campus meals, so budgeting could be pretty tight. She simply needed to tell her parents the cost so they could provide the necessary funds.

On her day of departure, Colleen gathered her things and hugged her parents before messaging for the transport vehicle that would take her to the high-speed train station. She opted to save the robot fee and load her belongings into the trunk herself before giving the command to proceed to the station. The electric vehicle left her neighborhood and soon joined the steady stream of driverless vehicles on the nearest major roadway. Few drove their own vehicles because of the cost and inconvenience; people-driven cars were relegated to separate lanes on roadways because of their greater risk. Driverless cars in the fast lanes were all designed to interact with the other cars to minimize travel time and ensure safe passage.

Colleen arrived at the station within minutes. She and her bags were scanned after she stepped onto the moving walkway that passed through the station security zone outside of the main entrance. This was necessary because, while the world was generally at peace, various international groups of thugs still presented a security threat to travelers and places where large groups of people gathered. Colleen was automatically shunted onto the walkway that entered the station after it was confirmed that she posed no risk. A few others were switched onto an alternate walkway for additional screening.

The biometric information gathered during the scanning was used to determine her destination, causing her to be shunted again, this time to the gate for her train. At the specified time, passengers were allowed to walk on their own to their designated cars and take their reserved seats. After loading her bags, Colleen dropped into her window seat and waited for the ride to begin. It would take about two hours to arrive at Northern, a distance of nearly 450 miles. Although not as fast as the tube or air travel, the high-speed rail option was still pretty quick and it offered greater comfort.

Colleen used her time on the train to consider the projects that she could do for Dr. Daniels. While not educated on any of the specifics of interpreting data collected from the multitude of telescopes and probes used in space exploration, she was a very fast learner and knew some of the basics from school. In addition, she had mastered the school's advanced math and science classes. The extent of her capabilities was better reflected, however, by her proficiency in ten or more languages. Colleen's interest in these languages was based largely on pattern definition, how the words and structures of the languages were similar. Because of her deficient social skills, however, she rarely had time to use these languages in direct communication with others. Overall, Colleen was confident that Dr. Daniels would find that she could do many things while at Northern.

As the train pulled into the Northern station, Colleen got her things together and prepared for the final, short leg of the journey. She navigated directly to the check-in location for summer interns; hers was just one of several programs hosted by the university. From there she was escorted to her room in the undergraduate dormitory, and then taken on a short tour of the campus. While she found this exercise tedious because of her advanced planning and complete memorization of the campus layout, she forced herself to be as patient and polite as expected.

After orientation Colleen hurried back to her room, settled in, and continued preparations for her first meeting with Dr. Daniels the following morning.

5

DIVING IN

"Hey, Jamie, how are those calculations going?"

"I'm nearly done, Dr. Daniels, but I want to double check before I hand them over to you."

"OK, but I'd like to wrap this up before noon so we can send our results to Dave."

"Got it," Jamie replied. "And you want both me and Min to meet the summer intern this morning, right?"

"Oh, gosh, I forgot all about that," Vera said. "Yes, yes, I'll need you both here. Yikes, it's in fifteen minutes!"

"Or even earlier," Jamie said, pointing down the hallway at a diminutive, young girl heading their way.

Colleen was so anxious to get started that she took the short walk from her dormitory to the astronomy building well before the scheduled meeting time of 10 a.m. One thing she learned from her parents was that arriving on time for a business meeting was really the same as showing up late. You needed to be there early. This approach, however, was foreign to many in academia who regularly appeared ten to fifteen minutes late or failed to show up altogether.

"Please intercept her and give me a few minutes to get ready," Vera said.

"Sure, I'll show her around," Jamie said. "She's really young!"

Jamie walked toward Colleen, greeted her, turned her around, and took her on a tour of the building. She first showed her the rooftop telescope, something used primarily for teaching now because it was so small and old. Colleen was unimpressed, disappointing Jamie, who had expected a "wow" moment. Jamie, like everyone else, underestimated Colleen because of her size and age. Jamie then took Colleen to see the lecture hall and lunch area before directing her toward the office she shared with Min.

Jamie and Colleen found Min head down analyzing data to determine the rogue planet's precise path. The Northern team served as the lead for five groups across the globe who were independently performing their own assessments of the planet's route. Redundancy on a matter of such importance as this was absolutely essential, and Northern would be responsible for adjudicating the final result. All involved knew that they simply couldn't afford to be wrong about where the rogue planet was heading.

"Min," Jamie said in a soft voice intended to not startle him, "I'd like you to meet Colleen, our summer scientist."

"Er, um, hi," Min mumbled, head still down.

"Min! She's over here," Jamie said, annoyed by his rude behavior.

Min looked up and cast his eyes upon Colleen. "Oh, I'm sorry, but I'm in a rush to get this done before noon." He stood up to greet her properly.

"Working on the rogue planet?" Colleen asked.

"Yes, you know about that?" Min replied, falling prey like everyone else to the tendency to underestimate Colleen.

"Of course," Colleen said. "I'm planning to help you, so I've researched the matter in great detail."

Colleen took a peek at Min's work and immediately noticed an error in his math. "You might want to fix that code," she said, pointing to the error. "I think the sign is wrong."

Jamie was amazed, while Min struggled between anger and embarrassment. He could tell that Colleen was right but didn't want to admit it.

"Oh, yeah, I knew that but forgot to make the change."

Jamie stifled a chuckle and did her best to help her partner recover.

"So, you've got a pretty strong math background it seems," she said to Colleen. "Tell us about the courses you've taken in school."

Min turned off his data display so there would be no more review, and Colleen gave them details on the math and science classes she had taken. Neither Jamie nor Min had skipped any grades in public school, so they were amazed to learn how far advanced Colleen was for her age.

"That's, that's amazing," Jamie said after Colleen had finished. "You're already prepared for college courses at your age. Fourteen, is it?"

"No, twelve," Colleen replied. "My parents don't think I'm ready for college yet, but there aren't many classes left, and we don't have a college near us for advanced courses. I've taken a lot of online classes but I'd rather be somewhere where I could do research while taking classes."

"Wow," Min said. "You're way ahead of where I was at your age."

Colleen said nothing but knew it was true. She also had the sense that she would be answering a lot of Min's questions before summer's end.

"Let's go meet Dr. Daniels," Jamie said. "She wants you there, too, Min."

The door was open when they reached Vera's office, the professor busy at her desk.

"Come on in," she motioned to Colleen. "You must be Colleen."

"Yes, I am," Colleen said. "It's great to meet you."

They shook hands and exchanged small talk before getting down to business. Vera could sense right away that Colleen had no interest in talking about her home, school, or other matters, so she quickly shifted gears to discuss the science program.

"This is the fifth year that Northern has hosted the summer science program," Vera began. "We take great pride in bringing young scientists here to learn and work with us on our projects. You'll get to spend a lot of time with Jamie and Min, supporting their work and learning some things about how we analyze astrophysics data. Any questions so far?"

"Will I get to help with your work on 217 and the rogue planet?" Colleen asked, using the shorthand for the name given the brown dwarf, Finder 217.

Astrophysicists were rarely creative when naming their discoveries. The planets were tentatively named 217 a, 217 b, and 217 c. Planet 217 c, or C, was closest to the brown dwarf, and planet 217 a was the closest to Earth. Even though Vera had announced the discovery of the brown dwarf system, scientific protocol required that this finding be confirmed independently by others. The rogue planet's existence, however, had already been confirmed by others, but it had not yet been named.

"Well, that's pretty advanced work, and the rogue planet is such a high priority that I don't believe we'll be able to let you get involved with it," Vera replied.

"I'm pretty sure I can help you, Dr. Daniels," Colleen argued. "I've done a lot of studying on those topics, and I'm pretty good with advanced math and coding."

Min cringed at the latter comment, but Jamie came to his rescue once again.

"She really does have a firm understanding of both projects," Jamie offered. "We talked with her briefly about them in our office. I'd like to see if she can help us with some of our calculations on the rogue planet. It's such a crazy timeline and we're under a lot of pressure. Any help is appreciated."

Vera yielded, saying, "Well, I'll leave that to you and Min to decide." Vera realized that she would have more free time for her own work if her students spent more time with Colleen. "Speaking of which, you should get back to your office so you can meet that noon deadline."

The two graduate students marched off to their office with Colleen right behind. Min was quite relieved to escape the discussion without proof of Colleen's math skills being provided. He had suspected she would talk about her discovery of the error in his calculations, and was pleased that she had not.

"OK," Jamie said after they settled in the office, "let's have Colleen review both of our sets of code to see what she finds. We'll also review each other's work to make sure there are no errors."

Colleen was seated in the middle chair between Jamie and Min at a long bench along the office wall in their spartan office. She quickly found several more errors in Min's work, much to his dismay.

"So, what's wrong with it?" he asked, pointing to one of the errors she identified.

Colleen explained what was wrong in each case, but didn't provide a solution, infuriating Min. He had to ask each time how to fix it. It seemed that Colleen loved to rub it into his face, but she was simply handling things like she always did, with no consideration of the other person's feelings. Colleen expected Min to be better at what he did. Jamie could sense what was going on, so asked Min to go to another professor's office to get some data she needed.

"Look, Colleen," she said after Min left, "it's great

that you're already helping to fix the problems, but you're upsetting Min in the process. He's put a lot of time and effort into the work, and errors are likely when you're under so much pressure."

"They were pretty stupid mistakes," Colleen said. "He should know that stuff."

Jamie bit her lip, not wanting to start things off poorly on day one with the young genius.

"Maybe so, but try to be a bit nicer," Jamie said. "That's all I'm asking."

"OK," Colleen said, thinking of this as just another one of those things she needed to do as part of her growth.

Min returned to the office in a better mood, and the morning progressed more smoothly thereafter. Colleen found no errors in Jamie's work, and, after final error checking, they delivered their work to Vera just before noon. Calculations from the other four groups arrived by the end of the day and Vera assigned Jamie the task of identifying and resolving any differences. The results were generally in agreement, but straddled the point where the rogue planet would cause problems in the Solar System.

Northern's analysis had indicated that there would be no problems, and Colleen was able to convince Jamie that their calculations were the most accurate. Two of the other four teams had also concluded that the rogue planet would pass just far enough away to not alter orbits in the Solar System, a factor weighing heavily on Jamie's decision to agree with Colleen. Jamie reported her conclusions to Vera, and, after some discussion, Vera notified the groups that the "no impact" conclusion would prevail.

Northern's press release indicated that the rogue planet would pass within three AUs of the Solar System, but that there was only a very small chance of an impact. It also reported that the rogue planet would continue to be tracked to ensure Earth's safety. The world breathed a collective sigh of relief at news of the finding, but those in the scientific community were still on edge because of the potential consequences of being wrong by even a very little bit. In their minds, the analysis was not done until the threat had passed, something that wouldn't happen for another twenty years. They would continue to take measurements and provide updates on the rogue planet's path until then. Politicians, however, were eager to accept the finding and direct their attention, and funding, to other matters.

6

MIN

Colleen was the first to arrive at the office the following morning. Now that the rush was over for delivering the calculations on the rogue planet, Vera's team would be returning to analysis of data on Finder 217 and its three planets. This project, too, was a multi-national effort. Dr. Daniels was the principle scientist for the Finder Mission, but she was only one of many involved in data analysis. Lòpez and Davids at Hawthorn Tech, for example, each had teams of scientists looking at various aspects of the spectroscopy and other data being generated by space probes and telescopes on Earth and in space. Additional telescope time was now devoted to that sector of the sky, and a few satellite missions were changed to turn their attention to the newly-discovered celestial bodies.

Colleen settled into her chair and began examining data that would be used to determine basic facts about the planets, including their size, mass, composition, length of days and years, temperature, and whether they had water and oxygen. She was excited by the project because she could apply her special ability to detect patterns in complex data sets. Without graphs or statistical analyses, she could see similarities and differences that others could take weeks to detect through complicated mathematics. She was hoping to determine which, if any, of the planets was most likely to support intelligent life. Such a finding, she thought, would justify sending humans to the planet, and she wanted to be on that mission.

Her assignment, however, was to simply organize information so Jamie and Min could do the analyses. They had laid out specific tasks for Colleen to perform before they arrived in the morning, tasks that Colleen had no interest in completing. Colleen was so wrapped up in her exploration of the data that she didn't start any of the tasks she was expected to do.

"Good morning, Colleen," Jamie said, entering the office at about 9:30. "Did you sleep well?"

"Hi, Jamie," Colleen replied. "Yeah, it was OK."

"I always hated sleeping in dorms," Jamie said. "Too much noise at all times of the night. It nearly made me crazy."

"Oh, it was pretty quiet last night after ten o'clock," Colleen said. "Our dorm is full of kids here for summer programs, and we have a strict curfew."

"You'll see how long that lasts, but it's good they're giving it a shot. Were you able to organize the data like we asked?"

"Oh, um, well," Colleen said, now remembering what her assignment was. "I, I just need a little more time to finish," she lied.

"That's OK," Jamie said. "I have a few things to do first, and I need to talk with Min about our plans before we get going on this. Just try to get it done within an hour and we should be fine."

"Sure," Colleen said. She immediately turned to the assigned tasks and nearly had them completed before Jamie returned from a coffee run.

Min joined them fifteen minutes later. They reviewed what Colleen had done and began their analyses. Colleen was given additional tasks to perform, completing them before lunch. She then spent her time peeking in on what Min and Jamie were doing. Jamie didn't notice that she was being observed, but Min was a nervous wreck, fearing that he'd make more mistakes that the smart-alecky young genius would find and broadcast to all who could hear.

Min was basically right, as Colleen couldn't keep quiet after seeing a few more errors in his work. Jamie had gone out for an extended lunch, so only Min and Colleen were in the office when the fireworks began.

"I'm getting tired of having you look over my shoulder," he said to Colleen. "Weren't you given an assignment?"

"Yeah, but I finished it," Colleen said.

"So, let me get you something else to do, or why don't you just go out and have your lunch?" Min said.

"I'm not hungry," Colleen said. "I can fix those mistakes you've made."

"What mistakes?" Min asked. "I'm not done yet. It's not your concern."

"Go ahead, then," Colleen said. "I'm sure Dr. Daniels will be happy to know that the planets will be bumping into each other like billiard balls each time they rotate around 217."

"What do you know about it?" Min said, angrily. "You're an expert on this now after one day?"

"Your coding is sloppy," Colleen replied. "Anybody with half a brain can see that."

This infuriated Min, who couldn't believe the cockiness of this little twelve-year-old. "Don't talk to me like that!" he snapped. "I don't care if you are a genius. You're acting like the little child you are." He got up from his chair and stormed out of the room so he wouldn't say anything else.

I'm the little child? Colleen thought.

Min walked toward Vera's office thinking that he would have a short talk with her about the precocious little child genius. Her door was open, but after reflecting for a moment, he didn't go in, deciding that he should probably cool off before having that discussion. As he started to walk away, he heard his name come up in a telephone conversation between Vera and Carla.

"No, I don't think Min will make it through the program," Vera said. "He just doesn't seem to have what it takes. He hasn't mastered the science and his math isn't strong enough. I'm not sure what to do about him."

There was silence as Vera listened to her friend's response. The two professors routinely confided in each other over a range of academic and personal issues. They both found it beneficial to have another person's thoughts on complicated matters, often changing their minds after they talked.

"Yeah, I hear you," Vera said. "That's what I'm thinking I should do, but you know it's always hard. He's a sweet kid and works hard. I hate this part of the job."

After hearing this, Min walked out of the building.

"Where's Min?" Jamie asked upon returning to the office.

"I don't know," Colleen said.

Min returned a couple of hours later and started packing up a few of his personal belongings.

"What's going on here, Min?" Jamie asked. "Are you going somewhere?"

"Yeah, I'm leaving the department," Min said.

"What?"

"I had a talk with Dr. Daniels, and we agreed that

this program wasn't working out for me." Min had, indeed, returned to the building and spent nearly an hour with Vera to discuss his predicament. He found that he was actually relieved by the decision to leave the department because it created new opportunities for him to consider. He didn't know yet what he would do next, but he planned to find something that would keep him involved in space exploration.

"So, just like that, you're leaving?"

"Yes. I need to find something else."

"Colleen," Jamie said, "do you mind if we have a little private time here?" She motioned for Colleen to leave the office.

"Why now?" Jamie asked, after Colleen had closed the door behind her.

"Why not now?" he replied. "Things aren't going well for me here, so it's time to try something new."

Jamie gave him a hug and then helped him with his things. She knew it was the right decision but felt sorry for him. He had been a hard worker and she valued his friendship. They shared a few laughs about some of the things they had experienced over the past couple of years in the department and pledged to stay in touch.

Colleen returned to the office shortly after Min had gone. She didn't notice that Jamie was upset.

"I can do the programming that Min was working on," she said.

Jamie didn't reply. Min's departure made her think about of lot of things, and programming was not on the list. She began to wonder about her own future, whether she was on the right path. She knew she was a shoe-in for a PhD, but then what? Would she go into academia, government, or industry? Would she stay involved in the space program or apply her skills in other areas? What about her personal life?

"Do you want me to do that?" Colleen asked, awakening Jamie from her musings.

"What?" Jamie asked, somewhat startled.

"I said I can do Min's programming."

"Well, I'm not sure Dr. Daniels would allow that," Jamie said, annoyed at Colleen's insensitivity to what had just happened to Min.

"Why not?" Colleen said. "This is easy for me."

"You're twelve years old and you're not a student or employee of the department."

"But I've already been doing it by fixing the stupid mistakes Min made."

Jamie was about to lose all patience with the precocious little genius. She steamed but didn't say a word, thinking how to best handle the situation. But she couldn't restrain herself, and spoke loudly.

"That's *exactly* the kind of thing I've heard you saying to Min, even though you've been here less than two days! Do you *ever* think about other people?"

Colleen was stunned because nobody had ever challenged her poor behavior. Her parents and teachers just tiptoed around it. Her classmates had seen it so much that they just tuned her out.

"Oh, I'm sorry," Jamie apologized, realizing that this was just a kid she was yelling at. "I didn't mean to yell at you, really."

"I, I didn't know that I had said anything wrong," Colleen replied, her eyes welling up with tears.

"Really?"

"Yeah."

"Wow, you come from a strange place," Jamie said. "Do you talk like that to your parents and friends?"

"I don't know. I just say what comes into my head. Don't people want to hear the truth?"

"Well, yes and no."

"What do you mean?"

"Sometimes the truth hurts, like with Min. Yes, he made the mistakes you found, but he put his heart and soul into his work. It's hard stuff for him. For you to just point out his errors and not give him credit for the good things he had done isn't fair. It's cruel."

"I thought I was helping."

"You were, but you made him feel like you were judging and belittling him. Think about it. You're *only* twelve and you spotted problems a 25-year-old graduate student had made. He has already been through four years of college and has studied for years and you just popped in yesterday. You're not even out of high school yet."

Jamie and Colleen talked more and, although she didn't really see what the big deal was with Min, Colleen made a conscious effort to learn from what Jamie was saying. Colleen, of course, would simply make mechanical changes to her behavior pattern, but maybe others would think she was being sincere.

Jamie decided it was time to pack up for the day, telling Colleen that she would talk to Dr. Daniels about letting her take on more advanced responsibilities. Colleen was satisfied with waiting for word from Dr. Daniels, and took some materials back to her dorm room so she could study more that evening.

7

SIGNALS

"Did you hear the news?" Colleen asked, excitedly.

"What news?" Jamie said as she dropped her bag on the desk. Colleen had been in the office for a couple of hours before Jamie arrived and couldn't wait to share what she had heard.

"The news from SUP!"

"What's SUP?" Jamie asked, before realizing how stupid that sounded.

"'Space Unites People,' the independent group that is part of the search for extraterrestrial intelligence," Colleen said, not seeing the humor in Jamie's question.

"Oh, that group of wackos," Jamie said, dismissively. "They are on the fringe of the SETI effort," she added, using the common shorthand for the "Search for ExtraTerrestrial Intelligence."

SUP was known to regularly detect "signals" from space, largely, according to skeptics, to keep the money coming into their organization. "Have they found Martians again?"

"No, they reported intelligent signals from the area where Finder 217 was discovered. There could be life there!"

Jamie, while scoffing at the report, was pleased to see that Colleen could show some true emotion. She hadn't seen her smile or be excited about anything since she met her a couple of days earlier.

"Well, not so fast there, Colleen," Jamie said. "That group has been proven to report false signals many, many times."

"I know that," Colleen said. "But this is different. Look at this." She pulled up a video of the news report and displayed it for Jamie. Although it seemed credible because the signal was very different from their past hoaxes, Jamie refused to accept it as fact. SUP's history was too full of false reports for her to believe anything they claimed.

"It needs to be confirmed by somebody else, preferably real scientists, before I or any other credible professional would accept that these are real signals," Jamie said. "I'm sure they're raking in the dough now, however. Nothing like an exciting new tale to generate contributions."

Colleen wasn't swayed by Jamie's arguments, largely because she wanted to believe that intelligent life could be found on those planets. She hoped that the news would create interest in sending a human, specifically her, to one of the newly-found planets. Normally guided exclusively by logic and available data, Colleen allowed her wishes and beliefs to govern her thoughts about intelligent life on a just-discovered planet.

Just as they returned to their work, Dr. Daniels poked her head into the office.

"Good morning," she said. "Do you two have a few minutes to chat about some news I've just heard?"

"Certainly," Jamie said, not fully prepared for what was to come.

"I've seen reports about intelligent signals coming from 217's planets," Vera said. "The down side is that the first reports came from SUP, and we all know how unreliable that group is."

Jamie nodded in agreement, while Colleen sensed that another shoe was about to drop.

"But," Vera continued, "it seems that there has been initial confirmation from a group in Spain. They report finding faint laser bursts originating from the center of one of the planets. I'm not sure what this means, or how accurate the findings are, but this will generate great excitement and new interest in our project. That can't be bad."

"Alright!" Colleen exclaimed in a rare outburst of joy.

"There you go," Vera said. "Excitement as advertised."

"Sorry," Colleen said, "but this is cool."

Jamie, a bit embarrassed at finding that her sarcastic statements about SUP had now been undercut by new facts, remained quiet as Vera launched into some ideas she had about expediting their analysis of the Finder 217 system. While she acknowledged that the loss of Min would hurt them in the short run, she was optimistic about getting some immediate help from two students mentored by another professor in the department. She added that she would also aggressively seek a post-doc researcher within the next few months, drawing from the large pool of recent PhD recipients who hadn't yet landed a permanent job.

"I know you'll have a greater workload until we get more people, Jamie," Vera said, "but I hope to make it a temporary problem."

"Speaking of that," Jamie said, deciding to use this opportunity to ask if Colleen could do more, "maybe we can expand Colleen's duties a bit so she can help out?"

"Oh, that would be highly unusual," Vera said. "She's just here for the summer program, and we've never had summer students take on responsibilities like that. You and I can discuss it in my office." She knew it was inappropriate to discuss the matter in front of Colleen and didn't want to disappoint or embarrass the young girl.

Jamie joined Vera in her office while Colleen went back to reviewing any information she could find on the three planets. Min had left a lot of data on his computer, so Colleen dove right in.

Vera and Jamie had a long discussion about the challenges of having a summer student do work that was normally done only by those with advanced degrees. In addition to her doubts that Colleen could do the work, Vera feared breaking both university and summer program rules.

"This isn't easy work, Jamie, even for graduate students like yourself," Vera said.

"I know, but Colleen was essentially doing Min's work before he left. She kept finding and fixing errors in his code."

"But how can she know what to do with no experience in our field?" Vera asked. "She's just a kid."

"She's not just any kid, Dr. Daniels," Jamie said. "She's a freakin' child genius, and she has incredible interest in what we do. She's studied the topic nonstop and can dance circles around many of those who've been in the field for years."

"Well, I'm still not sure. Let me check with the department head and summer program administrator to see what they think about this. In the meantime, test her out a bit by having her do the exact same analyses you are doing so we can compare results and see how capable she is."

"That sounds good to me," Jamie said. "Thanks,

Dr. Daniels."

Jamie returned to the office, gave Colleen some analyses to complete by day's end, and offered to answer any questions she had. She expected, however, that Colleen would finish the assignment in record time, asking only whether there was something else she could do while waiting for Jamie to finish.

Colleen quietly developed the code and ran every analysis that Jamie had requested, coming up with estimates of the sizes and masses of the three planets. She finished within an hour or two and looked over to see that Jamie was completely immersed in her own work. Colleen decided to take advantage of the opportunity and look into the spectroscopy data which should indicate whether the planets had water and oxygen. There hadn't been a big rush to look at the spectroscopy because the data were just beginning to come in. Colleen had only limited experience with spectroscopy in high school, enough to know that it was a technique to determine the composition of matter based on how it absorbed or emitted different wavelengths of light. There were many different spectroscopic methods, so she first did some research on those used in astronomy.

Jamie finally finished her analyses in late afternoon. She asked Colleen to provide the products of her work and then walked to Vera's office to compare results. It didn't take long to confirm that Colleen could handle the work.

"Amazing," Vera said. "I knew she was smart, but this is way beyond my expectations."

"You've never had a student genius before?" Jamie asked. "I mean, other than me, of course."

Vera smiled at the obvious joke and told Jamie that she had never even worked with such a talented individual, let alone taught or mentored one. This was a whole new experience, and she wasn't quite sure how to handle it.

"Let's just enjoy the ride," Jamie said. "She's a bit of a pill, but her brain is unbelievable. We could get way ahead of the pack with her helping this summer. And her name will look cute on our publications."

"Now, don't get ahead of yourself, Jamie," Vera cautioned. "This was impressive work, but we don't know how broad her knowledge and skills are, so we need a plan to make sure we don't have her do things beyond her capabilities."

"Yeah, I understand."

"So, I want you to develop an approach to validate a portion of her work. You can't check it all, but you need to check enough, say ten percent, so we know she's not drifting."

"OK."

"And I want you to check the results the first time she does any new type of analysis."

"Alright, even with that, I think we'll get a lot more done than if I did it alone."

"I hope you're right. I got approval from both the department and the summer program to let Colleen do the work. I agreed to ensure that this won't stress her out. Please keep an eye on that, and let's make sure we have some fun things for her after hours. We need to keep her healthy."

"Got it," Jamie said. "I'll have a plan for you tomorrow morning. By the way, too bad about Min."

"Yes, it is, but I think a change is best for him."

"He didn't tell me his plans. Do you have any idea?"

"As a matter of fact, I do. He expressed interest in engineering, something to keep him involved in space."

"Cool," Jamie said. "Maybe we'll see him again down the road."

8

BROWN DWARF PRESS BRIEFING

"Today I'll give you an update on our findings regarding the brown dwarf, Finder 217," Vera said to the small group gathered in the Astronomy Department auditorium. She had given many briefings before, but didn't particularly care for them, mostly because what she said was often twisted and messed up by the time it appeared in the news or popular publications. In the past, she had followed up with reporters to have them make corrections, but she no longer bothered.

Vera gave a quick recap of the initial discovery of 217 and its planets before launching into a discussion of what they had learned since then. Her typical approach to briefings was to be as precise as possible and then provide a simplified version for those who couldn't understand the details.

"Because brown dwarfs never ignite like hot stars

such as our Sun, they don't emit light in the visible range. We therefore use infrared spectroscopy to study them. This has been going on for decades, and we now have quite a catalog of information on brown dwarfs, a sort of fingerprint collection that we use to characterize them. We compare the infrared spectra with those in the collection to see if we can find matches." She cast an image of an infrared spectrum and explained its features and what they meant.

"We were able to find a reasonable match for 217 and used that to provide some basic information about the brown dwarf. We've also estimated the distance to 217 using what's called the parallax method. Let me illustrate."

She cast a diagram showing how infrared images of 217 taken six months apart could be used in concert to calculate its distance from Earth. "While it's difficult to make precise measurements of the angles from Earth to the stars, the trigonometry is simple." Few in the grouped followed this because many had either not taken trigonometry classes or had forgotten everything they had learned about it. Vera pressed on.

"How did you find the planets? There are three of

them, right?"

"Yes, there are three planets that we know of. We used Doppler spectroscopy for our preliminary findings."

"What's that and how does it work?"

Vera had prepared well for the briefing, pulling up another image, this one illustrating application of Doppler spectroscopy. "Dr. Carla Lòpez from Hawthorn Tech did this work. Her team detected a shift in the infrared spectrum emitted by Finder 217, thereby indicating that there were likely planets in orbit. The observation period was quite short, however, so they didn't have sufficient data to develop clear patterns in the spectrum that would confirm the tentative finding." She went on to explain that a Doppler shift was like hearing the pitch of a siren change as an ambulance approaches and moves away from you. Planets can be indicated by such shifts in the infrared spectrum from 217 because the planets tug on the brown dwarf, causing it to move back and forth relative to Earth.

"So, you don't really know if there are three planets?"

"Well, technically, you're right, but we have very strong evidence to indicate as much. We just need to perform additional tests to confirm what was found from the Doppler spectroscopy. That's typically how it goes."

"But wasn't there a very recent report about laser signals from the vicinity of 217? Wouldn't that support the planet theory?"

Because only a few in the room had heard about the SUP discovery, the room was quickly abuzz with questions. Vera, not being directly involved in the work, opted to deflect and recommended that they ask SUP or members of the team from Spain that confirmed the findings.

After a few more questions about the methods used in their research, Vera glanced at the clock and saw that the one-hour time limit was rapidly approaching. She would soon be free again.

"So, to summarize, we know that 217 is a brown dwarf near the edge of our Solar System. We also believe that there are three planets in orbit. We know little else, and that's what we're working on now." Seeing several hands in the air, she knew she couldn't escape just yet. "OK, one last question."

"Like what? What are you working on?"

"For example, we'll estimate the mass of 217 using gravitational microlensing. That's a method derived from Albert Einstein's theory of general relativity. Essentially, we measure how much the brown dwarf bends light coming from a distant star to either Earth or a telescope in space. The greater the bend, the greater the mass. It's not always possible to do this because you need a bright enough star in the right place, but we got lucky. Jamie Bishop, one of my PhD candidates, is working with data collected by a space telescope operated by India for this analysis. This is one of several space telescopes now pointed at 217."

Vera thanked those in attendance and promised other briefings in the coming weeks as they gathered new information. She then attempted to leave the room, only to be trapped into additional discussions by a few reporters who lingered. Despite her pleadings for years, facilities management refused to provide a back-door escape route from the auditorium. She knew this was a losing battle because several of her more gregarious colleagues argued that it would be bad form to slip out the back. After finally freeing herself from the last reporter, Vera hurried back to the privacy of her office.

9

STILL A CHILD

Colleen was now working so efficiently that Jamie had to work overtime to keep her end of the bargain with Vera. The young genius generated five times as much output as a normal person. Still, Jamie found enough time for her own analyses that their combined efforts resulted in a small catalog of basic information about the 217 system within just a few days. Not wanting to surrender major findings to other research teams, Vera had directed them to use all of the data they could get from their work and the work of others. The race to publish was on!

Colleen had picked up on Min's work regarding the planets and their orbits. Jamie was busy organizing and analyzing the space telescope data from India. Her analysis of Finder 217's mass was nearly finished.

Colleen combined data from Carla's team with new data in an attempt to confirm that there were three planets. Fortunately, the planets were so close to 217 that their years were very short, providing more data points to detect periodic signals in 217's spectrum. Colleen envisioned the complex pattern in her head before confirming with computer analysis. Additional scrubbing of the data would be required, however, before the orbits of each planet could be nailed down.

At week's end, Vera sat down with Jamie and Colleen to review their work. She was once again impressed by Colleen's capabilities, and amazed by the amount that she had accomplished in less than a week. This experiment with a child genius was working out very well so far.

"So, what do you want us to do next?" Jamie asked.

"Well, I think we need to clean up the work on the mass of 217 and the confirmation of its planets," Vera said. "I'd like to have some additional photometry, more measurements of the brightness and color of 217 over time. That will help us nail down the mass. The likelihood that we are correct about the planets is greater because we believe we've found three, but that's not good enough. We need to rule out other possibilities, including, for example, whether the signal dips we see result from true planet transits instead of spots on 217. I don't think we have enough to make an announcement."

"Really?" said Colleen, annoyed and disappointed that they couldn't keep marching forward with additional analyses. She wanted to examine the new spectroscopy data to further dissect the composition of the atmosphere on 217 and the planets. She wanted to find evidence that the planets could support life.

"Yes, really," Vera said. "You can't just rush through these things, Colleen. We need to be doubly sure of our findings before we go public. Anything short of that is foolish."

Colleen slumped in her chair, a reminder that she was still a kid. Vera chose to ignore her behavior because she simply didn't have time for it. Instead, she continued discussing her expectations for the next several days.

Jamie, sensing a need to lower the tension, suggested that the three of them take a break and have dinner together at a nearby restaurant. It was 5:30 on a Friday, and there were very few people still in the building. Vera remembered her pledge to keep it fun for Colleen and offered to pick up the tab. Colleen grudgingly joined them, although she preferred to keep working with the data.

Dinner was an eye opener for Vera as she saw "the pill" side of Colleen. With the exception of a short discussion about Tulip, the young girl could not talk about anything other than the work they were doing. She lacked any gracious manners and ate only a few basic foods, refusing to try anything other than her limited repertoire. Vera could not tell if the dinner actually achieved her goal of relaxing Colleen, but she did learn that Colleen was an unfinished product in many ways. Perhaps working with a child genius was not as wonderful as it had first seemed.

10

PUSHING

Colleen grinded through the analyses that Vera had requested, not because she thought they were necessary, but because she wanted to move on to the spectroscopy data. Her immediate objective was to provide scientific backing for the SUP findings so she could argue for a human mission to 217's planets.

With Jamie's help, Colleen had provided sufficient documentation of the planets' existence and their orbits within days. After Jamie had determined the mass of 217 with acceptable confidence, Vera made a public announcement of their findings. Scientific journal articles would follow, but Colleen was most interested in moving forward with her search for intelligent life.

Colleen concluded from her subsequent analyses that planet C was a serious candidate for intelligent life. She found evidence of an Earth-like atmosphere and a reasonable temperature range on

C. In addition, she detected only low levels of radioactivity coming from the brown dwarf. Because she had only a few weeks left in her summer program, she worked hard to develop enough information to convince Vera to make the case for a human mission to C before she left. Colleen hoped that this would start the ball rolling on a mission she could lead several years later.

Jamie, however, was less focused on finding human life than she was on getting her PhD and starting her professional career. She worked with Colleen on the brown dwarf analyses, but did not help her make the case for intelligent life on C. Her dissertation, the lengthy report summarizing her research, was based on 217 itself, not the planets. Because the dissertation was a major requirement for earning her PhD, Jamie's primary interest, by default, was centered on the brown dwarf and its properties.

"Dr. Daniels, we need to have a human mission to C," said Colleen, bounding into Vera's office.

"Sounds good to me, Colleen, but that's a huge mountain to climb," replied Vera. "The competition for funding is nuts and a mission to C would be incredibly expensive. We're still just touching the tip of the iceberg on C. It's hard to argue for such an expensive mission with so little information."

"What do you mean, 'so little information'?"

"Everything we suggest about the presence of life is based on preliminary analyses. That won't be enough when arguing for financial commitments from SSEA," said Vera using the acronym for the Space Science and Exploration Agency.

"But everything, including signals from the planet, points to intelligent life," Colleen argued. She and Vera both knew that multiple observers, including SUP, had concluded that the laser bursts were likely to be coming from C.

"I understand your passion, Colleen," Vera said, "but you need to try to see the big picture. It's not just about you or me and what we think or believe. These are huge decisions affecting many people and a *lot* of money."

"That is *exactly* why we need to fight for this."

"You're a genius, and I mean that, but you are still just a kid. How do you think it would look if I argued to spend billions of dollars on a mission because a twelve-year-old thinks we'll find life on the planet?"

"Maybe it would look like you are a genius, too," Colleen said without thinking.

"Darn it, Colleen, that's why it wouldn't fly. You act like the child you are at the most inopportune times."

"But I'm right, and you know it."

"No, I *don't* know it, and that's the problem. Look, I'll put a proposal together that includes the human mission as an option. That's the best I can do now, and that will be a lot of work for me. These proposals are very demanding, and I'll need your help to fill in some details. I'm not optimistic about the outcome, but I'm sure you'll have chances to push for a human mission during your career. By then, we'll have better data and you can make a much stronger case."

"I *will* be on a mission to C," Colleen said.

"Somehow I think that's true. I hope I get to watch."

11

PLANET C PRESS BRIEFING

Vera and Jamie presented findings from their recent publications on 217 and its planets at a press briefing attended by representatives from leading scientific publishers. While credited in the papers, Colleen was no longer at Northern, the summer program having ended months earlier.

"Yes, Colleen Freeman, our summer intern was invaluable to us on this project. She truly is a genius with a very bright future ahead of her."

"Can you tell us more about her contributions?" The line of questioning was frustrating to Jamie because she expected to be the star of the show, having just recently earned her PhD from Northern.

"Sure," Vera said. "We know that brown dwarfs have often been found to have significant levels of methane and water in their atmospheres. Colleen examined the spectroscopy data and found a substantial amount of water. She also analyzed spectroscopy data for the three planets and found evidence that planet 217 c, or C, has a dense atmosphere similar to Earth's atmosphere."

"And other work she began indicated that there was ozone in the planet's atmosphere and that Finder 217, the brown dwarf, emitted low levels of x-rays," Jamie added. "All of this is favorable to life. Since her departure, we've learned that C orbits at about 0.02 AU from 217. This means that the planet's temperature may be about the same as that on Earth."

"How frequently does C orbit around 217?"

"Our current estimate is once per week," Jamie replied.

Vera and Jamie answered several more questions before Vera publicly congratulated Jamie for receiving her PhD. The warm response from the press erased any hard feelings Jamie had due to the earlier questions about Colleen.

"That's all we have for you today," Vera said. "We'll have additional briefings as our findings warrant. Thank you."

12

MISSION

FIVE YEARS LATER

"Colleen? This is Vera Daniels."

"Oh, hi, Vera."

"How have you been?"

"Doing well. I'm close to my dissertation defense. Two more weeks."

"Fantastic!"

"Yeah, Dave said I've got it locked in," Colleen said, referring to Dave Davids at Hawthorn Tech. "Just need to dot the i's and cross the t's."

"Great. I have some good news for you after that."

"What?"

"SSEA has approved the human mission to C."

"Really?"

"Yes. Another long-range mission was scrapped due to engineering issues, and we were next on the list. Additional funding is still needed, but we were given approval to move ahead with planning and design. You probably know that signals from C have continued and there is growing interest in checking it out."

"Yeah, I do."

"I hope you're ready for flight."

"I've already done some of my SSEA training, so, yes, I'm ready!"

PART II

13

NEARLY READY

FIFTEEN YEARS LATER

"OK, let's get this thing up in the air," Qadira Nagi said. "People are waiting – on both planets!" She and others on the Mission Team were meeting in California to discuss final preparations for Encounter 1, the historic mission to C.

It took a decade to plan Encounter 1 and build the spacecraft. The spacecraft, named the "Nellie Bly," was the largest ever built, so large that it had to be launched as multiple segments to be assembled in low Earth orbit. Nellie Bly was a famous pioneer who began a 72-day journey around the world in 1889, an unheard-of adventure for females back then.

The lander segment would carry C Lander, the spacecraft that would land on and later launch from planet C. The command segment, Com, would carry astronaut Colleen Freeman and two robots. The robots would take over command of the Nellie Bly, or Nellie, whenever Colleen slept or needed a break. They would also control Com when Colleen was aboard C Lander. The habitation segment, or Hab, was the largest segment and would have artificial gravity and house the food gardens, exercise equipment, Colleen's quarters, and water and oxygen supplies. It would also hold a small, cryogenically-frozen puppy to be revived as necessary to ease the loneliness that Colleen would most likely suffer during the planned 29-year mission.

Qadira was the design engineer for Nellie. Her company, QN Space Exploration, was the world's top contractor for space-based missions. They currently had the largest and most reliable rocket available, the QN X, surpassing even those created by the legendary Elon Musk, who led one of the first private companies to develop spacecraft for government missions. The QN X could lift over 600,000 pounds into low Earth orbit and would be used to launch both the Hab and C Lander segments. A much smaller rocket, the QN IV, would be used to launch the lighter Com. Despite decades spent on researching alternative methods such as nuclear propulsion, the most reliable rockets for human flights still used chemical propellants like liquid oxygen and kerosene. Efficiencies had been gained, however, and these rockets could achieve greater lift and speed with the same amount of fuel as rockets used in the previous century.

Testing of the rocketry had been completed, but there were still logistics issues to work out for the supply and docking aspects of the flight. The bold flight plan involved using gravity assists from Mars, Jupiter, and Moriarty, the name given to the newly-found rogue planet. It had been named after James Moriarty, the arch enemy of Sherlock Holmes, the still-admired private detective from centuries long past. Astronomers, apparently, still had some sense of humor.

"We need final calculations on the gravity assist from Moriarty," said Jamie Bishop. She had become the Mission Manager a couple of years earlier, after Vera Daniels retired due to health issues. Vera was only in her mid-sixties, but was unable to handle both her position at Northern and the demands of managing Encounter 1. Jamie had not envisioned this sort of role after obtaining her PhD, but there were few projects as interesting as the C mission. Vera had been more than happy to have Jamie work on the mission, and Jamie rapidly rose to the number two position and was the obvious choice to replace Vera.

"So, how are we doing with our flight window now?" Colleen asked.

"We're still on schedule for the launch," Jamie said.

"I'll be ready," Colleen said. She had earned her SSEA flight certification since obtaining her PhD at Hawthorn Tech, and after five years of mission training, was impatient to get started. Besides having unparalleled knowledge and understanding of C, Colleen was also a small but healthy package for flight, at 5'3" and 110 pounds. Flight engineers loved that she required little space, added only a small amount of mass to Com, and would be easy to feed from the crops and foodstuffs loaded into Hab. Her bland diet was also a plus given the limited options for preserved space foods.

"Are the robots ready?" Jamie asked.

"RB and LB are ready and excited to get on with it," Frances Kelmar said. Frances had spent eight years developing these two robots to simulate the right (intuitive, thoughtful, and subjective) and left (logical, analytical, and objective) brains of humans. Because Colleen was known to be lacking somewhat in right brain capabilities, RB was considered the more important of the two robots. Both, however, would be essential for confirming calculations and decisions Colleen would make as the mission progressed. Signals to and from Earth would take so long later in the mission that Control Center responses to difficult questions would typically come too late, and robot assistance would be needed.

"What about Janus?" Colleen asked, referring to the third robot that was named after the ancient Roman god of doorways, beginnings, and endings. Janus would be located inside C Lander at launch and would be used primarily to handle tasks specific to activities on C.

"We're very close. Testing yesterday revealed a few small bugs in the code. We'll have it fixed in a couple of days."

"OK, let us know ASAP." Jamie then progressed through every aspect of the mission, taking the better part of two days. Various teams specializing in launch preparations, communications, navigation, environment, food and water supply, and other aspects of the flight appeared during their allotted time to provide status reports. Twenty years after Colleen had essentially shamed Vera into setting forth a proposal for the mission, they were just a couple of months away from launch.

Jamie gave Vera a call after the meeting to keep her informed. She had pledged to tell Vera as much as she could as things progressed, keeping her involved in what was likely her last space adventure. Vera and Jamie had grown closer over the past few years, the student-teacher relationship from Northern now a deeper, true friendship. Vera was still the mentor, but Jamie was fully capable now of handling things without her. Jamie just didn't want to.

Colleen was a different story, however, and her relationships with Vera and Jamie hadn't progressed much beyond where they were when she was twelve years old. There was no animosity or professional rivalry of any sort, but the warmth and friendship that could be expected after so many years of working together hadn't developed. Colleen was still so focused on the science that she had little time for anything else. This was considered an asset by many associated with the mission, because they believed it meant she was unlikely to get lonely over time. There was nobody to miss, and no history of interpersonal relationships to engender longing for others while on her journey. Some, however, argued that this lack of essential humanness made her a poor representative for the first encounter with intelligent alien life. Jamie and Vera saw both sides of the argument, but hoped for the best.

14

PRE-HAB LAUNCH PRESS BRIEFING

"Good morning. I'm Jamie Bishop, Mission Manager for Encounter 1. Here with me today are Qadira Nagi, Nellie's design engineer from QN Space Exploration; Dr. Colleen Freeman, Nellie's Commander; and Dr. Frances Kelmar, who designed the three mission robots. We will give you an overview of the mission, talk about the specific components of Nellie, and give you a sense of what Dr. Kelmar's robots are prepared to do."

Jamie then cast a holographic presentation that could be seen by all in the room. The first slide depicted the flight path for Nellie. She then showed a mission timeline.

"It's been a long time getting to this point, but, as you can see, we are only a day away from our first launch. Qadira will talk more about those details. We'll be sending parts of the spacecraft up into low orbit for several months, with the expectation that Nellie will be ready for the mission in two years. Once it leaves Earth orbit, Nellie will swing by Mars and Jupiter for gravity assists to increase speed and also send the spacecraft up toward Moriarty, the rogue planet. Moriarty is about three AUs above the Solar Plane, as you can see from the illustration. An astronomical unit, or AU, is the distance between Earth and the Sun. We've never flown spacecraft on such a path, but that poses no special concerns. We need to use Moriarty for a huge gravity assist to bring Nellie's speed up to 400 kilometers per second, a new record for human space flight. At that rate you could fly from New York City to Honolulu in twenty seconds. Despite that high speed, however, the total mission time is estimated at 29 years. The very young Dr. Freeman, here, will no longer be a spring chicken when she returns." This comment drew chuckles from many, including Colleen.

"How do you know enough about Moriarty to do a gravity assist? Won't that be dangerous?"

"Good questions," Jamie replied. "We are pretty sure that Moriarty is a gas giant like Jupiter and currently estimate its mass to be about eight times that of Jupiter. We'll have time to gather additional, better data on its mass and speed as Nellie approaches. We'll fine-tune our plan after we have the best data. It's always dangerous to do a gravity assist because you have a risk of crashing into the celestial body. There is also a risk of shooting past the body into deep space. We've used Jupiter and the Sun many times for gravity assists, so have a lot of experience that we'll apply to this mission."

"I'd like to turn this over to Qadira Nagi now," Jamie said, before sitting down.

Qadira gave a quick overview of her company before describing the spacecraft. She used a rotating three-dimensional image to identify each of Nellie's main parts. Next came a simulation of the launch and assembly of the Hab segment.

"Hab will be the first segment launched, as I'm sure you know by now," Qadira said. "It could not fit inside available launch vehicles fully assembled, so we decided to deliver it in quarter-sections to low Earth orbit with four launches in the same month. A construction crew will be shuttled back and forth between Hab and a nearby space station for assembly, a process that we expect to take about nine months. Testing and stocking Hab with supplies will follow construction."

She next described the lander segment, noting that

engineers had designed C Lander so its rockets could be used for both landing and launch.

"Even though gravity on planet C is only about half that on Earth," Qadira said, "the payload has to be minimized and optimized to keep fuel needs down, while still providing the supplies and equipment Dr. Freeman will need to explore C. In addition, unlike the Lunar Module used more than a century earlier for the Apollo missions to the moon, C Lander has to be able to withstand severe forces and temperatures similar to those encountered in an Earth reentry. Other than the fuel needed to begin the trip home, perhaps the most valuable part of the payload on C Lander is the robot, Janus, which will be in command whenever Commander Freeman leaves the craft for exploration. Dr. Kelmar will talk more about the robots."

Qadira then turned her attention to the command segment, Com, which would carry Colleen and her two other robotic companions. After responding to several questions about specific functions of Hab, C Lander, and Com, she moved on to a discussion of how the spacecraft would be assembled and tested in low-Earth orbit.

"Com will be launched eighteen months from tomorrow to allow time to first ensure that all things are satisfactory on Hab. Engineers will check systems and prepare Com for docking with Hab. The lander segment will be launched only if all things are go after Com and Hab have docked. For you history buffs, the segments will be assembled in a manner similar to that used for the Apollo missions of long ago. C Lander will be docked in front, with Com and Hab following in sequence, as you can see in this simulation. After final checks, Hab will fire its thrusters to launch Nellie on its way to C. Straight forward, right?" There were several smiles in the audience, but equally prevalent were looks of bewilderment. This was a very complicated ordeal, generating many questions that Qadira answered in full detail.

"What about testing of the various features of Hab? How did you do that?"

"We took that very, very seriously because Hab is essentially a huge life support system for Dr. Freeman. Any food that is not preserved will be grown there, and the main water and air supplies will be kept and processed for re-use there. All waste products will be processed there. In addition, Hab will house exercise and entertainment equipment and devices, as well as the cryogenic chambers and quarters for the Commander. There are many requirements, so the opportunities for failure are abundant. We performed rigorous testing on all systems of the fully-assembled Hab before it was disassembled into quarter sections for the four separate launches. We'll test them again after it's reassembled in space."

"OK, now for the fun part," Jamie said after Qadira answered her final question. "Dr. Kelmar will talk about the robots."

Frances stood and looked back as the curtain behind their seats opened up. Lighting revealed three small robots who then quickly joined her on stage. The press was awestruck.

"Please let me introduce you to our three robots, RB, LB, and Janus," she said, pointing to each as they were named. "LB is our left-brained robot, and she is programmed to be logical, analytical, and objective. RB is our right-brained robot, and he is programmed to be intuitive, thoughtful, and subjective. Janus has all of the capabilities of the other two robots, and also has additional programming unique to the C Lander. Janus will take over controls when Commander Freeman is exploring planet C."

"Why a separate left brain and right brain? Wouldn't it be better to give each robot a whole brain?"

"That's very perceptive," Frances said. "We spent a lot of time with space psychologists to determine the best way to program the robots. They agreed that it would be best to create LB and RB as separate sides of the brain so Commander Freeman could have a focused discussion with one side or the other. She herself is very much left-brained, so the ability to communicate solely with the other half might benefit her in certain situations. Don't forget that this is a very long mission and she will likely have times when she just needs to deal with an entirely logical or entirely emotional matter."

"What if one of them malfunctions during the mission?"

"We can reprogram the other robot to take on any characteristics and capabilities needed. In fact, we've already pre-programmed the robots to have all characteristics and capabilities, but suppress some to create LB and others to create RB. All three robots, by the way, can perform a wide range of physical tasks both inside and outside of the spacecraft."

"Are these the real robots that will be on the mission?"

"Ha, there's always a smart one in the crowd," Frances said, chuckling. "You're right. These are test versions. The others are in sterile settings until the launches. LB and RB will go up with Com, and Janus will launch with the C Lander."

"Are we ready now for the star of the mission?" Jamie asked, referring to Colleen. "Dr. Colleen Freeman is the Mission Commander, so we'll have her say a few words and answer a few questions. We've run late, so let's make this quick. You'll have other opportunities to talk with her before Com launches."

Colleen provided a fairly drab presentation, noting her interest in C but not giving any background from her early days at Northern. This was fine with Jamie, who wanted nothing more than to end the long briefing and resume working on mission details. The press members were clearly exhausted as well, as none had questions for Colleen, and several appeared more than ready to bolt for the door. They were well aware of their opportunity to quiz Colleen later, and some were also well informed about her general lack of personality. On this day, she was viewed by many in the room as the least interesting part of the mission.

15

FIRST LAUNCH

"We launch tomorrow," Jamie said. "Can you make it here?"

After a brief silence, Vera said, "I'll be there."

Jamie provided Vera with the details on how to check in at the launch facility. This wasn't Vera's first launch, but procedures at the Virginia site were different from those at other locations. Vera would be among a group of about thirty individuals given VIP guest status, many of whom were long-time colleagues. She was too frail to ride in the tube and, ironically, didn't like to fly, so she booked a high-speed rail trip to Assawoman on the main line from Wilmington, Delaware, to Norfolk. The Assawoman stop was added years ago when the launch facility at Wallops Island had to be moved inland because of sea level rise caused by global warming. Since the move, the Assawoman site had grown to become the largest of SSEA's launch facilities.

The launch dates for Hab had been in jeopardy for several months as a seemingly endless string of technical issues had arisen during ground testing. For example, the rotating cylinder designed to generate artificial gravity was found to be unstable. In addition, the hydroponic garden was losing too much water. Testing also revealed many problems with both the air quality sensors and the automatic responses to problematic conditions such as low oxygen levels.

Although there were a large number of problems to address before launch, mission scientists and engineers had anticipated issues due to the complexity of the systems on Hab and the very low tolerance for failure. They would try to address all problems before Nellie left Earth orbit, but also developed a plan for performing emergency repairs in Mars orbit if necessary. There were no repair facilities beyond Mars, however, and a return to the Red Planet after slingshotting around Jupiter would doom the mission because of the fuel required for such a reversal.

Jamie and other mission managers were in constant communication as pre-launch diagnostics were run and reported out. It was four hours before launch, and Vera had made her way to the launch facility. Jamie quickly greeted her before returning to the Control Center.

Vera then boarded a small bus for the ride to the observation area for VIPs. It was the last bus to depart, and she was thrilled to see so many long-term colleagues as she walked to the back to occupy the last available seat. The bus was alive with chatter, and Vera's spirits were elevated by the unabashed enthusiasm they showed for the launch. Everyone on the bus was aware of the many possibilities for failure, but they also knew that they couldn't do anything about it. They trusted those in the Control Center, many of whom they knew from previous missions, to make the right choices for a successful launch.

Stepping off the bus after a short ride, Vera walked to the observation building. Those who had taken earlier buses were already gathered and chatting, with an eye toward the new arrivals. Vera quickly spotted Colleen and ambled over to talk with her.

"Hi, Colleen, how are you?" Vera said.

"Vera, I didn't think you'd be here," Colleen replied.

"I wasn't sure I'd be here either," Vera chuckled.

"How have you been?"

They talked briefly about Colleen's job at Barkley Technical Institute where she was now an assistant professor. That career would end with the launch of Com the following year, but her role at the Institute was already largely assumed by others because of the amount of time she had to devote to the mission. While still not a warm and engaging person, Colleen had matured enough to develop some awareness of those around her. She asked Vera about her health.

"I'm hanging in there," Vera said. "Some days are better than others, and this is certainly one of those good days. I'm really excited about the launch, and seeing all of these familiar and new, young faces inspires me. How are you handling your preparations?"

"I'm ready to go," Colleen said matter-of-factly.

"Is it really that simple for you?" Vera asked. "I mean, you'll be gone for 29 years, alone in space." Vera quickly realized that, while her facts were correct, this was the type of insensitive statement Colleen would make. "I'm just, well, I'm just amazed at your strength."

"I've wanted to go to C ever since I learned about it that summer at Northern," Colleen said. "I have a chance to see things nobody else has even imagined."

"But do you worry at all about being lonely?" Vera asked delicately.

"I'm alone most of the time anyway," Colleen said. "That's how I get things done, how I think about things. No, I don't think that will be a problem. Besides, I'll have three robots and a dog for company."

"Well, there *is* that," Vera chuckled, but, before she could continue, Colleen was diverted away to speak with others in the crowd. Vera worried about "her" child genius, wondering if her cold nature would harm her more than hurt her in deep space. She would have few happy memories of friends and family to draw upon during the long journey. There would be no soft smiles or spontaneous laughter associated with glimpses of people she loved or funny things they did together. She did not have typical memories, and that concerned Vera. She also had difficulty imagining how a possible encounter with intelligent alien life would go. While Colleen represented the very best of human minds, her insensitivity was nearly equally exceptional.

"Vera!" said Carla, tapping her on the shoulder.

"Hey," snapped Vera at being suddenly jolted from her thoughts of Colleen. "Oh, I'm sorry Carla," she said after recovering and recognizing the smiling face of her trusted colleague.

"You seem to be halfway to C," Carla joked.

Vera laughed and the two old friends quickly caught up with each other. As they were talking, the launch time approached and observers were taking their positions to see the rocket go off.

"Ten, nine, eight, seven, six, five, four, three, two, one, LIFTOFF!" they screamed as the rockets fired and the sound-suppression mist billowed below. The mighty QN X rocket lifted straight up with a stream of flames shining brightly against the clear blue sky. The shock wave that passed through the observation area seconds after the launch reminded the VIPs of the rocket's raw power. They watched as the reusable booster separated and later turned to the monitors to watch it land on a nearby recovery pad. The launch had gone perfectly, and the first quarter-section of Hab was on its way into space.

16

POST-LAUNCH PRESS BRIEFING

"Good afternoon," Jamie said. "I'm very happy to announce a flawless initial launch of Hab quarter-sections. You may be aware that there had been a few technical issues that we had to overcome in ground testing. For example, engineers had to devise a fix to stabilize the rotating gravity cylinder. We also found issues with water loss in the hydroponics garden, a problem solved by adjusting the technique and selection of crops. Finally, we re-designed air scrubbers and filters to address air quality problems."

"That's a large number of serious technical issues, Dr. Bishop. Does that imply a high risk of failure during the mission?"

"There is always risk in space flight," Jamie replied, "but we believe we've minimized these risks, not only with the fixes I described, but with the overall approach to both the mission and design of the spacecraft. We established a very low tolerance for failure from the beginning."

"What was done to fix the artificial gravity cylinder?"

"The instability was caused by both a lack of rigidity in the structure and the uneven and varying distribution of weight in Hab. Our engineers strengthened the structure and improved the mechanism for managing weight distribution dynamically to minimize wobble."

"Can you describe a bit how you can both grow crops and provide the water needed by Dr. Freeman over a 29-year mission?"

"Sure," Jamie said, casting a diagram illustrating the water cycle for the mission. "As you can see, the only source of water is what we put on the spacecraft before launch. Capture and reuse, therefore, are essential to our strategy because water has a huge impact on the overall payload. In short, water is heavy to lift, so we limit the amount as much as possible and do what we can to keep it all useful on board. Dr. Freeman will consume about three quarts of water each day, and plants, of course, will require a constant supply of water. As they grow, these plants will need even more water.

And we need to provide a comfortable level of moisture in the air. Our systems are designed to maintain a sixty percent relative humidity in both Hab and Com for the entire mission. The Lander will only be humidified during use. This air quality demand increases the overall water requirement. Water vapor released by Dr. Freeman and the plants will certainly contribute a little bit to humidity, of course, but additional water is needed to maintain the desired level. We performed extensive computer modeling on the water balance and found that we need to keep total water loss in Hab under fifty percent for the mission to ensure all needs are met. That sounds like a lot of loss, and it is, but it amounts to just a few drops per gallon each day. We believe we've adjusted everything we can to easily meet that goal."

"You mentioned relative humidity, but isn't there a risk of toxins accumulating in the air as well?"

"Yes, that is always an issue with space flight," Jamie replied, swapping the water cycle for an illustration of the air quality system design. "The first plan of attack is to minimize the number of toxic materials on the spacecraft, and we've done that based on our decades of experience. The filters and scrubbers I mentioned will handle whatever toxins do contaminate the air. For humans, there is the additional requirement to keep oxygen levels high enough and carbon dioxide levels low enough at all times. Dr. Freeman will need nearly two pounds of oxygen per day, and there will be additional needs for the cryopreserved puppy. We've calculated a need of about ten tons of oxygen for a 29-year mission."

"Won't the plants provide some oxygen?"

"Yes, plants will provide some oxygen by converting carbon dioxide, but that's a small contribution overall."

"What about converting water to oxygen and hydrogen through electrolysis? Hasn't that been proven to work?"

"Yes, that is a proven technology, but the oxygen contribution would be a small part of our needs and would also increase the water requirement. So, we've equipped Hab with a sufficient supply of oxygen to address all mission needs. Air quality monitors in the spacecraft will track conditions and automatically adjust the flow of air through the filters and scrubbers to maintain a safe environment."

"What about nitrogen? Doesn't nitrogen constitute 78 percent of Earth's atmosphere?"

"Yes, that's right," Jamie said, "but the human body doesn't need nitrogen. We are, however, using nitrogen to maintain cabin pressure."

"Will you be using any caches on the trip to provide supplies during the journey?"

"That's another good question, but, no, we won't," Jamie said. "Missions to Mars have benefitted from having 'cache' spacecraft at multiple locations between Earth and Mars, much like the stashes of supplies used by mountain climbers and early explorers to the poles here on Earth. But for Encounter 1 there is little overall benefit to using caches so near Earth because the journey is extremely long. We will be using Mars as an emergency stopping point, however, if Nellie experiences major problems that would prohibit it from reaching its destination. We could make some repairs using staff and supplies that we have positioned on Mars settlements."

17

MORIARTY RETURNS

All four quarter-sections of Hab were successfully launched into orbit within the planned four-week timeframe. It took nine months to connect them to create the Hab module. Testing and missions to supply Hab were completed in another eight months. According to the master plan for Encounter 1, Com would launch in 28 more days with Colleen aboard. A new discovery, however, would jeopardize the mission.

Dr. Lòpez had found an error in the calculations that led to the conclusion that Moriarty would not affect the outer planets of the Solar System. Dave Davids, now the SSEA Director, announced to the world that Moriarty was once again a threat to the Solar System. Its path needed to be altered to ensure that Earth would not be endangered by shifts in the orbits of Saturn, Neptune, and Uranus.

"Did Moriarty change course?" Colleen asked in a

meeting with Jamie, Dave, and Carla.

"No, we think the original calculations were off a bit," Carla said. "I'm very sorry to say this, and I know it has to hurt. The error was miniscule and incredibly difficult to find."

It wasn't just her friendship with Vera, but also her unwavering respect for the work done at Northern over the years that caused Carla great pain to make this statement. She had no doubt that the original calculations were imprecise, however, as the new calculations had been repeated multiple times by various universities around the world. All of the results agreed this time. Jamie was shocked and Colleen stared in disbelief.

"Are you absolutely sure about that?" Colleen asked in a sharp tone.

"Yes," Carla said, not wanting the discussion to escalate into an argument. She was well aware of Colleen's continued shortcomings in interpersonal skills. Although much better than when she was younger, Colleen still had some very rough edges.

"Assessing blame is counter-productive," Dave said. "We need to focus on what can be done to avert disaster. The whole world, literally, is counting on us now."

"That's right," Carla said, "and I know we have the capabilities on this team to get it done."

"Yes, yes," Jamie said in a weak voice, "we need to figure out how to stop Moriarty." She felt deep responsibility for the error because she knew that she had the lead on the calculations. Colleen had been a kid at the time, so it wasn't her fault.

Colleen felt humiliated, because deep down she believed that it *was* her fault. Sure, Jamie had final responsibility, but they all knew that Colleen was the most intelligent, despite her age. She was the genius, the wiz kid. No matter how you cut it, Colleen was ultimately responsible for putting survival of the Earth in jeopardy. Thinking ahead, she also knew it put the Encounter 1 mission at risk.

"We all know Nellie is our only option," Colleen said. "We need to add Moriarty to the mission."

"*Add* it?" said Dave, incredulously. "I don't think we can afford to look for alien life if the cost is the destruction of Earth. We need to completely change the mission."

"What if we can't save Earth?" Colleen asked. "What then?"

"You're right, Colleen," Jamie said. "The two missions go together."

"Right," Carla said. "We'll need a place to inhabit if we can't stop Moriarty, and C is the best option we know of."

"You're all crazy," Dave said. "We can't do both."

"I think we can," Colleen said. "We need a way to shift Moriarty's course when Nellie approaches for the gravity assist. After that, Nellie continues on to C."

"Exactly," Jamie said.

"So, how do we budge Moriarty?" Dave asked. "Is there a rocket big enough?" He knew there wasn't.

That's when the room fell silent. Nobody had an immediate answer, yet they all knew it would take incredible force to move a planet so large, even the infinitesimally small amount required to prevent it from skirting too close to the Solar System.

"Let's meet tomorrow with Qadira and others to see what's possible," Jamie said.

"OK," Dave said. "Jamie, please put together a group of experts to assess our options."

"Got it."

The importance of the task ahead was not lost on any of those in the room. They filed out determined to find a solution to their planet-sized problem.

18

MORE ROCKETS

"It's pretty clear that Nellie is the only option we have to reach Moriarty and alter its course," Dave said to the assembled experts. "We need to move it just enough so it doesn't affect the orbits of our outer planets. So, what can we do with Nellie to push that monster out of the way? That's our challenge."

"Phew, that's a tall order," said Lebron King, a top spacecraft designer who often worked with Qadira on projects. "Isn't Moriarty bigger than Jupiter?"

"Yes, about eight times more massive," Colleen said.

"What type of force will be required to do that?" Min asked. After leaving the Northern astrophysics department, he had found that his skillset and interests were best aligned with rocket engineering. His career had taken a very positive turn, including designing the most powerful nuclear fission reaction rocket, or FRR, that was now available for space flights.

"Glad to see you again, Min," Jamie said. "We go way back," she said to the others in the room. Min smiled.

Colleen recognized Min, but simply observed him without a welcome. She didn't see the point in reminiscing, and, if she did, the memories would not be confidence builders for her. She didn't think highly of rocket engineers, especially Min.

Qadira took the lead in running through the numbers on how much force would be required to budge Moriarty. Colleen concurred with her estimates, which quieted the room.

"My FRR doesn't even come close to providing a millionth of that force," Min said after a long period of silence. "I could maybe move a large asteroid, but huge planets are out of the question."

"Maybe I can help," Carla said. "I've just discovered an asteroid, perhaps fifty miles across, in the plane of Moriarty. We don't have enough data yet to publish, but I brought what we have to get started here. Our surface maps are preliminary."

"So?" Min said.

"It's currently on a course that takes it near Moriarty," Carla said.

"And you want to alter that course so it hits Moriarty and solves our problem," Colleen said.

"Brilliant!" Dave said. "Can we do it?"

Carla provided data on the mass and path of the asteroid so Colleen could do some rough calculations on the possibility that the plan would work.

"An FRR can't do it," Min said after hearing the estimate of force required to move the asteroid. "We'd need five."

"Only two will fit into Hab with the other stuff already loaded," Qadira said. "And we don't have time to unload it."

"Nor do we want to," Colleen said.

"Right," Jamie said. "Two missions."

"Let's tow them on a space barge," Lebron said matter-of-factly. "And let's bring six for a safety margin."

A space barge had never been used before. The concept had been explored for previous missions to Mars and various moons in the Solar System, but it was abandoned each time because better, proven options were found.

Lebron had been involved in the latest proposal to build a space barge and was well-versed in their design. He developed some quick sketches of what it would look like and how it would be attached to Nellie. He also presented some ideas on how it could be packed into a rocket for launch. Qadira expanded on his ideas and gave specifics about which rockets could be used for the mission. Because she believed that the payload was relatively small, she recommended the QN IV and said her company could have one ready within a few weeks.

"But we'll need to launch the FFRs separately and mount them on the space barge in orbit," Lebron cautioned. "That means two rockets."

"And the second rocket needs to be your most powerful," Min interjected. "The FFRs are very large."

"OK, then," Qadira said, "we'll have a QN X ready as well." Lebron and Min nodded their approval.

With no other good options on the table, the group agreed that Lebron would move forward on the space barge and Qadira would prepare the rockets for launch. The Barge, as it would be called, would carry six FRRs that would be remotely landed on the asteroid at strategic positions. The FRRs would be adjusted and fired from Nellie, providing a sustained push to crash the asteroid into Moriarty. Carla would gather more data to improve on the crude surface maps she showed. Min would manufacture the FRRs, enhancing their capabilities if possible, and developing the system for remote operation.

"When can we have this ready?" Dave asked.

"Six months," Lebron replied without hesitation.

"OK, but we can't afford any delays," Dave said.

"You won't have to," Lebron said confidently.

"We have a lot to do," Dave said. "I'll need all of your help on this. Are you available?" Dave looked around the room.

"You've got it," Colleen said, speaking for the entire group. Every person at the table knew that there was no more important thing for them to be doing.

19

NEW MISSION PRESS BRIEFING

"You all know that Hab has been launched, assembled, and tested. We were then ready to launch Com, but the Moriarty problem reappeared. Unfortunately, our calculations on its path were slightly off."

"So, who made the error in calculating Moriarty's path?"

After a short pause, Jamie said, "To be honest, I did. I made the error."

"Not true," Colleen said, approaching the stage. "It was my error. I'm responsible."

Jamie was momentarily stunned by Colleen's appearance, but recovered quickly to reply, "But I agreed with your recommendation. You were just twelve years old at the time."

The room was silent. Jamie had expected to be alone for the briefing, but Dave had been concerned that the event could get nasty for her. Colleen had appeared at his suggestion, and Dave followed right behind her.

"The error didn't cause the problem with Moriarty," Dave said. "Further, our normal scientific review process discovered the error. So, armed with a new assessment, we've changed the mission. That's how it works. It isn't always easy. Dr. Bishop, you were saying?"

Taking his queue, Jamie then proceeded to described how the revised mission would include a Barge from which Colleen would fire rockets capable of moving an asteroid into Moriarty. Members of the press hurriedly took notes and asked many questions about the details of this fascinating mission. Communication devices across the globe were abuzz with the story. Buried in the noise was the fact that Colleen had rapidly transformed from being the only boring element of a good mission, to being the source of a major scientific blunder, to being the potential hero of the planet. Her public acceptance of blame had taken her to new heights in the eyes of both the press and public at large, and she had instantly morphed into someone whom everyone could trust. And now she would put her life on the line to save every person on Earth.

20

TEAMWORK

Everyone involved was reasonably comfortable with the speed and trajectory Nellie would have due to the gravity assists from Mars and Jupiter because these assists had been done many times before. Nellie's approach to the asteroid and the landing and firing of the FRRs were much more complicated tasks, however. The spacecraft had to reach the asteroid at the precise location and time for landing the FRRs at the right locations. In addition, the rockets would need to be oriented properly before firing to ensure that they would provide the timing, speed, and trajectory needed to budge the giant rogue planet from its current path.

Min was busy tweaking the design of the FRRs to adapt them to this seemingly impossible task. Once the rockets were landed on the asteroid they could not be moved again. The direction of thrust from each would be fine-tuned on the ground after landing, but maximum efficiency and the success of the mission would require that the landing targets were hit within a quarter mile. Even with the additional data collected from redirected satellites, Carla was able to produce only slightly more detailed maps of the surface. Very little was known about relief on the asteroid, presenting a major challenge for landing the FRRs on a potentially craggy surface. To address this challenge, Min was working with Qadira to design landing systems that would be able to adjust automatically to variations in relief. To top it off, the FRRs would also need to be embedded in the asteroid's surface to ensure consistent, controlled thrust. Min could not count the number of times he banged his head against the wall because Lebron had boldly stated the job could be done in six months. Lebron's task, in retrospect, seemed much simpler than Min's, yet Min was not asked about his own timeline.

Lebron, meanwhile, was having great fun designing the Barge. Within two weeks, he had developed the basic design, how it would be folded up to fit within the QN IV, how the FRRs would be attached to it, and the mechanism for docking the Barge to Nellie. Qadira had collaborated with him and was simply amazed at how easily Lebron handled the challenge. Her rocket was ready for assembly at the launch location as Lebron's team started building the Barge. He would easily meet his six-month deadline.

"How is it going with the mass calculations on Moriarty and the asteroid?" Jamie asked Carla and Colleen, who were refining estimates on factors related to moving the monster planet.

"We need to get the error margins down a bit more," Colleen said. "We're at five to ten percent now but can do a little better."

"Right, there's too much wiggle in it now," Carla added before she and Colleen returned to their office to complete the task. Jamie strode over to Dave's office.

"What happens if Colleen misses her targets with the FRRs?" Dave asked Jamie. "What then?"

"Well, then we send her on to C and hope she finds friendly intelligent beings or no beings at all so we can begin resettling Earth's population," Jamie replied.

"We don't have the capability to do that, and you know it," Dave said. "We're just sending one human on Nellie. How are we going to send twelve billion people to C?"

"I don't think we'll need to worry about that right

now," Jamie said. "Call me naive, but I think we'll get this done."

"OK, you're naïve," Dave said, smiling.

"I didn't sign up for this," Jamie said. "I entered this field for the discovery, not to save humankind, at least not in this way."

"Yeah, I know. None of us did. Back when I first met Vera, her excitement about finding new planets and stars was absolutely contagious. She inspired me to work my tail off to make my own discoveries."

"She is quite amazing," Jamie said thoughtfully.

"How is she doing now?" Dave asked. "How's her health?"

"She's getting older, Dave. Her mind and spirit are there, but she may not be around for too many more years."

"Perhaps she's going out at the right time," Dave lamented. "I'm not as optimistic as you are."

"I'm really sorry I messed up on the Moriarty calculations," Jamie said.

"You didn't change the facts," Dave replied. "It just took longer for us to find them out. I put a lot of pressure on a lot of people to give me answers fast. I panicked and I regret that."

"It's not your fault," Jamie said. "You *found* the freakin' monster."

"Hmph, I was a rising star. I kept driving to be in the spotlight. Finding Moriarty should have been enough, but I then created the drama around seeing if it would destroy Earth. It should have been assessed quietly and reported after we knew the answer."

"We all compete, Dave."

"I took it too far. My craziness resulted in a twelve-year-old reviewing calculations that would predict the fate of humanity. I pushed too hard and rushed the whole process."

"She wasn't your typical twelve-year-old. Cut yourself some slack."

"Only if you do the same," Dave replied.

"OK, and you need to be more optimistic," Jamie said. Dave smiled.

21

OPENING UP

FIVE MONTHS LATER

"We're ready to go," Jamie told Dave.

"Right on schedule," Lebron added.

"I appreciate all you've done," Dave said to the assembled group. "This was an impossible task, yet you delivered. I firmly believe," he continued, now looking directly at Jamie, "that this mission will succeed and we will save the Solar System from certain disaster." Jamie nodded in approval, happy to see that Dave now shared her optimism.

"OK," Jamie said. "Com will launch tomorrow, followed in one week by the Lander and another by the Barge and FFRs. Everything will be launched from Assawoman so the Mission Team doesn't need to relocate. Any questions?"

There were no questions. Roles and responsibilities had been clearly laid out and everyone involved was well aware of the overall flight plan. One by one, they approached Colleen and gave her words of encouragement. She would begin the journey in mid-afternoon on the next day, an adventure that she had wanted to undertake for nearly two-thirds of her life.

"Are you all set to go?" Jamie asked Colleen.

"Absolutely," Colleen replied without hesitation. "Will Vera be here?"

Jamie was surprised by this question because Colleen was anything but sentimental. *Was she fearful of the journey? Did she regret that half of her life would now be spent alone in space?* Jamie wasn't sure how to react, so simply answered the question.

"She's here already," Jamie replied.

"I'd like to see her," Colleen said.

Jamie took Colleen to the hotel where Vera was staying. The three had lunch together outside, before Jamie returned to the launch site, giving Colleen time to visit alone with Vera.

"You've got quite a journey ahead of you, Colleen," Vera said. "You continue to amaze me.

Will your parents be here?"

"No, Dad died in a car accident, and my mother is in a care facility," Colleen said. "She's not been right since the accident, and never seemed to recover from the shock."

"That's too bad. I'm very sorry."

"They never really cared, so it's no big deal," Colleen said.

"Is that why you wanted to see me?" Vera asked. "Do you feel alone?"

"Hey, I passed all of the psychological testing, so don't worry about me," Colleen replied.

"Oh, I'm not worried."

"Then what?" said Colleen.

"You tell me."

Colleen was in uncharted territory. She did not expect Vera to see through her, to see that she needed something to hold on to while she was on the mission. She needed to know that someone would miss her, that someone would think of her as something other than the astronaut on Nellie.

Vera looked directly at her, and Colleen fought off the tears until the floodgates opened.

"Oh, Colleen, I'm here for you," Vera said as she held Colleen's head close to her chest. "I've always been here for you."

"I know, I know," Colleen said, wiping the tears away. "I'm not scared, and I'm not afraid of being alone."

"But you want to know that somebody is thinking about you the whole time, right?"

"Yeah, I guess so."

"Well, my dear Colleen, there are hundreds of people you know who will be thinking and caring about you throughout the mission. Just because you don't reach out to others doesn't mean they don't care about you. They do. Trust me."

Colleen tried to compose herself, somewhat ashamed at pouring out her emotions. Vera comforted her and let her know that it was normal to experience such feelings before a major life event. And this was an adventure unlike any ever taken before by a human being. She would be gone for 29 years, alone in space. Of course, she was feeling emotional.

"I probably won't be here when you return," Vera said.

"I know that," Colleen replied. "You're 67 now, right?"

"Yes, just under twice your age," Vera said. "Nobody in my family has lived past 85 as far as I know, so 96 is very unlikely."

"I want to thank you," Colleen said.

"For what?"

"For taking me at Northern when I was twelve, and for trusting me to help with your projects."

"Oh, I didn't trust you," Vera said with a smile. "I had Jamie double-check everything you did. I wasn't about to let a twelve-year-old run free with my science."

"Yet, you let me try."

"Yes, I did. I had never before encountered a child genius and didn't know how to handle it."

"In my opinion, you did just fine," Colleen said.

"Thank you."

Colleen leaned over to hug Vera but didn't quite know how to do it. Vera, sensing her difficulties, reached over and squeezed Colleen tightly. No words were spoken, or needed.

22

PRE-COM LAUNCH PRESS BRIEFING

"Hello, I'm Jamie Bishop of SSEA. I'm joined today by Dr. Colleen Freeman, Mission Commander for Encounter 1. Currently all systems are go and Com will launch tomorrow, followed in one week by the Lander and another by the Barge and its rockets. That's all I want to say before questions."

"What's it like to be the hero for an entire planet, Dr. Freeman?"

"I don't think of myself as a hero, and you shouldn't either," Colleen replied. "In fact, I haven't done anything yet. I'm fortunate enough to be the one flying Nellie, but the many people who developed the flight plan and designed and built the spacecraft are the true heroes. Dr. Bishop could be that person if she wasn't so blasted tall." Both Jamie and the press chuckled at this comment. While not particularly tall, Jamie was several inches taller than Colleen and far taller than the typical astronaut.

"How will you handle being alone for 29 years? Nobody has ever done that."

"Well, some would argue that I've already lived alone for 34 years," Colleen replied, eliciting more chuckles from the press and surprise from Jamie, who hadn't expected Colleen to be a charmer. "I know what's been written about me, but it's just who I am. I don't dislike being with people, but I find so many things to be fascinating that I just migrate toward those pursuits and, as a result, away from people. In space, I'll still have contact with people. Communication may be awkward at times due to transmission delays, but I will have contact."

"And you'll also have three robots and a puppy if you like," Jamie added.

"Yes, that's true," Colleen replied before deadpanning, "and that should be … interesting."

"It's my understanding that you've wanted to visit planet C since you were twelve years old. How does it feel to be on the verge of achieving that goal?"

"Well, I wouldn't call it 'being on the verge' given that it will take over fourteen years to get there, but it is exciting. I want to thank Dr. Vera Daniels for believing in me enough at that age to put forth a proposal for the mission. Yes, it's been changed to deal with Moriarty, but it all started with her. We wouldn't have the spacecraft to deal with Moriarty if Dr. Daniels hadn't pushed for a mission to C."

"What do you want to tell the people of Earth as you embark upon this mission?"

"Um, wow, that's a big question. I'm not sure what to say." Colleen glanced back at Jamie who encouraged her to give it a try.

"Well, I think I just want them to know that I'll do my best. It's no secret that planet C has been my greatest interest, but I will do all I can to take care of Moriarty. I'll never give up on that, and I know that I have a great support team in Dr. Bishop and the people at the Control Center. We're all in this together. I want to land on C knowing that everybody at home here on Earth is safe."

"This seems to be a good stopping point," Jamie said. "Thank you all for your continued interest in this mission. We'll keep you posted on progress as we move forward."

23

COM

It was now launch day, and the countdown clock was slowly ticking away. Com was perched high atop the QN IV rocket, cleaned and prepped for Colleen. The launch pad was readied and cleared of all nonessential personnel. The robots LB and RB were locked into their seats. The launch team performed checks on the rocket, communication systems, tracking systems, and other flight systems. All systems were go at this point.

Colleen had proceeded methodically through her pre-launch routine and was now ready to board Com. The liquid-cooled, pressurized launch suit felt heavy on her small frame, but the discomfort would be temporary. An assistant strapped her into her seat at the controls, and then exited through the hatch. Over the next hour Colleen and Jamie's Control Center team would perform final systems checks.

"Hello, LB," Colleen said.

"Good afternoon, Commander," LB said.

"Hi, RB," Colleen said to her other robot companion.

"Howdy, Colleen," RB said.

"Are you both ready for flight?"

"Roger," the robots said in unison.

"So am I," Colleen said. "It's time to get moving."

The propellants were then loaded into the fuel tanks. The main engines would soon fire and Com would lift off on its journey to be united with Hab.

Vera waited anxiously at the observation area with Carla, other scientists, and dignitaries. While the rocket was less impressive this time, the payload was much more interesting. In all of the excitement surrounding the plan to use an asteroid to change the orbit of Moriarty, many overlooked the second part of the mission. Earth would be sending an emissary for what could be the first-ever meeting with an intelligent alien life form. Vera bristled with pride, knowing that her young friend Colleen was the Earth's ambassador. Either part of the Encounter 1 mission was spectacular on its own, but the combination made this mission by far the most ambitious human undertaking ever.

Vera was hoping to be around long enough to at least know that Colleen had arrived safely at C.

Jamie was busy in the Control Center making sure all system checks were completed and everyone was ready to carry out their tasks. She had many assistants on the launch team, each managing various aspects of the mission. Dave and experts like Qadira, Lebron, Min, and Frances Kelmar were there as resources, but would have no direct roles in the launch.

"OK, looks like we're ready to resume countdown," Jamie said. A hold placed at T minus ten minutes confirmed successful fueling and satisfactory launch timing.

Excitement in the observation area was muted compared to the earlier Hab launches. The newfound importance of the mission was sobering for many in attendance. They believed they had only one shot to save the planet, and they were clearly on edge. The launch was successful, but many remained uneasy as Com lifted gracefully into the sky. Colleen was on her way on the journey of a lifetime.

"Well, she's off now," Jamie said to Dave as others performed their duties in the Control Center. "The lander goes up next week followed by the Barge and FRRs the week after."

"The game is afoot," Dave said to Jamie, making a play on the name "Moriarty."

"You know Sherlock Holmes never actually said that in any of the books, right?" Jamie replied.

"I still like it," Dave said, smiling.

Jamie gazed at the flight tracking monitor. "I wonder what she's thinking."

"Right now? Not much," Dave said. "She's too busy with communications to have time for herself. After she's established orbit she'll have a little time, but even then, I think she'll be too busy to reflect on the mission."

"Maybe that's a good thing," Jamie said.

"I think you're right. Even for Colleen, this could be a very emotional experience."

Jamie nodded and rejoined the activities in the Control Center.

"We have second stage separation."

"Roger," Colleen said.

Things were still going smoothly as Com achieved the orbit needed to dock with Hab. Although this was her first mission, Colleen had prepared so well that she anticipated every command and maneuver beforehand. LB and RB were simply along for the ride for now.

Docking with Hab was completed after the first full day in space. Colleen then instructed LB and RB to help work through the checklists to ensure that everything was operating correctly on both Hab and Com. No issues were found and Control Center continued with its preparations to launch the Lander in five days.

The Lander was launched on schedule atop the QN X. Once again, the flight went off without a hitch. There was a slight delay in the launch of the QN IV carrying the Barge due to a communications problem, but it was otherwise flawless. The FRRs were launched into orbit the following day. Two weeks after Colleen had launched, and about eighteen months after the first quarter-section of Hab was lifted into orbit, all of the parts for Nellie were ready for final assembly and testing.

The Lander was successfully attached to Com's nose within a day, and then the Barge was secured to the back end of Hab. The six rockets were then carefully mounted inside the Barge. Within two weeks, all testing had been completed, and Nellie was declared ready to leave Earth orbit.

"Now for the hard part," Dave said to Jamie.

PART III

24

NELLIE

Colleen had adjusted quite well during her first four weeks in space. As Dave expected, the constant communication with the Control Center kept her so busy that she didn't have much time at all to reflect on the mission ahead. She had become better acquainted with her robot companions while carrying out procedures to ready Nellie for the long journey, and they seemed to be a natural complement to her.

"LB, RB," Colleen said over Nellie's communications network, "it's time to fire up the rockets for escape velocity. Take your positions."

"Roger that, Commander," LB said.

"OK, got it," RB said as the two robots hustled from Hab where they were tending to the gardens. They used their small, built-in thrusters to navigate quickly through the airlock to Com. After they settled into their seats and checked all systems, Colleen informed the Control Center that they were ready to fire the rockets to leave Earth's orbit.

"Three, two, one," was broadcast from the Control Center.

"Fire!" RB hollered, startling Colleen and causing laughter in the Control Center. LB simply ignored the outburst which was clearly programmed by Kelmar to create some levity.

"That Frances Kelmar is crazy," Jamie said to Dave. "Who knows what else those robots will be doing to keep Colleen on her toes."

"I think it's great," Dave said. "Colleen will need some diversions to stay sane in that flying can."

It wasn't long before Nellie reached the escape velocity of 25,000 miles per hour, more than 122 football fields per second. Several in the Control Center believed they heard a muted "Yeeha!" from RB.

"Nellie is now on its way to new frontiers," Jamie announced. "Dr. Freeman, LB, and RB, you are the hope of planet Earth, and we give you our complete and unwavering support as you charge forward to grapple with the evil Moriarty."

"Roger," Colleen said. "And then it's on to C to meet some new friends."

Jamie smiled reflectively, recalling the time 22 years ago when Colleen insisted that Vera should propose a trip to planet C. She remembered doubting the report from SUP that signals were coming from the newly discovered planet. Colleen's instincts were right back then, and Jamie hoped that nothing had changed since. Although they had a detailed plan mapped out to handle Moriarty, Jamie knew that they would have to go off script at some point to address unforeseen circumstances. Because of the time required to communicate back and forth with Nellie in deep space, Colleen would need to make split-second decisions based on her judgment and anything LB and RB could provide.

"A bit melodramatic today, aren't we?" Dave said, reacting to Jamie's announcement.

"Perhaps," Jamie replied, "but you know as well as I do that we don't have a serious Plan B."

"Yeah, this is big," Dave said. "Real big."

"She *is* our best hope," Jamie said. "The folks on C may not like her much, but there's nobody I'd rather have taking on Moriarty."

"I'm counting on RB to loosen her up a bit," Dave said, chuckling.

"So far, so good," Jamie replied.

"Well, robots, we're on our way now," Colleen said to LB and RB.

Although they looked exactly the same, other than the "LB" and "RB" imprinted on their chests, Kelmar had programmed RB to have a male voice, while LB had a female voice. This distinction was made so Colleen could tell which robot was talking, but it also provided a human touch in an otherwise sterile environment. Every other contrast between the two robots was based on general right brain-left brain differences and specific programming created by Kelmar, some of which was designed to ward off the boredom Colleen would undoubtedly experience on her journey.

"Two years to Jupiter," Colleen mused, before turning her attention to more immediate concerns. "Have you two finished with the garden?"

"Garden is doing fine," RB said.

"Check," LB added.

"OK, take a look at the cryo chamber and the exercise equipment," Colleen said. "I'm going to need to use the gym a lot over the next 29 years."

LB and RB returned to Hab and went directly to the cryo chamber containing the preserved puppy. They checked the equipment settings and readings to ensure that the temperature was maintained at 320 degrees below zero Fahrenheit. After checking the puppy's vital signs and confirming that the liquid nitrogen supply was satisfactory, they viewed the puppy on the monitor that was fed by three small cameras in the chamber.

"She's cute," RB said.

"A subjective assessment having no merit," LB said.

"Colleen will like her," RB said, "and so will we, I think."

"That is not important to the mission," LB said.

"Colleen needs to have companionship to stay happy on this long mission," RB said.

"Happy?"

"Cheerful, merry, jolly."

"I know what it means," LB said. "She does not need to be happy to accomplish mission goals. I am not happy, yet I am able to perform all functions as needed."

"You're not human."

"I do not boast."

RB shook his head and gave up the discussion. The two then moved on to the exercise equipment, most of which had not been used yet. LB sat on the stationary bike and slowly pedaled to see how it functioned. RB took a quick glance at the resistive weight training machine and proclaimed it in suitable condition.

"Unsatisfactory assessment," LB said. "Without testing, we cannot determine its condition."

"Looks fine to me," RB said, concealing the fact that he didn't really know how to use the machine.

"Test it," LB commanded.

RB grudgingly attempted to comply, grabbing

hold of a long bar and pushing it up. Nothing. He then tried to push it down. Nothing again. He then adjusted a dial, setting it to zero. Pushing up again, he slammed the bar against the stop, causing his whole body to shake. He then let go and the bar came crashing down to the other stop.

"Like I said, looks fine," RB said timidly.

LB had moved on to the treadmill, checking the exterior and then standing on it with her back to the control panel. RB slipped in behind her, tripped over a cord, and landed on the start button. LB flew into the padded wall just beyond the edge of the treadmill.

"Treadmill functioning normally," RB said as LB pulled herself up from the floor.

"I am not happy," LB said.

25

DAY 1 – PRESS BRIEFING

"Hello, everyone. Nellie is now on its way," Jamie said. "All systems are functioning properly. Today, I'll recap what's happened over the past four weeks and give you a glimpse of what's to come in the near future."

Jamie quickly reviewed the Com launch and its docking with Hab, following by the launches of the Lander, Barge, and FRRs. She cast a simulation showing how the final parts of the spacecraft were assembled. Finally, she showed video taken by a nearby satellite as Nellie fired its rockets to leave Earth orbit. After responding to several technical questions, she moved on to discuss future activities.

"Nellie will reach the vicinity of Mars in ninety days. If all goes well, Nellie will just use Mars for a gravity assist toward Jupiter. Otherwise, as we've mentioned before, we will consider parking Nellie in Mars orbit for repairs, if needed, before moving on. We already have technicians and supplies stationed at Mars."

"Yes, we are limited in what can be done at Mars," Jamie said in response to a question about repairs. "In the worst-case scenario, we keep Nellie in Mars orbit until we can shuttle additional parts and supplies to it from Earth. We've prepared for that possibility, but hope that things go well and Nellie just flies by Mars."

"Wouldn't a stop for repairs jeopardize the timing of the Moriarty mission?"

"Yes, depending on how long it would take, we could find that our ability to strike Moriarty with the asteroid at the desired location would be compromised. That's a huge hypothetical, but we're prepared to do whatever we can to achieve our goals. Don't forget that there are twelve other nations with launch capabilities that are prepared to help us out if needed. Several already have spacecraft ready to go."

"What are the odds of sending such a huge spacecraft through the Asteroid Belt without getting hit by anything?"

"The odds are very good. Keep in mind that the

average distance between objects in the Asteroid Belt is nearly a million kilometers. We could probably go through sideways and still have less than a one-in-a-billion chance of hitting something. Still, we are using the latest data and best scanning equipment possible to track the positions of known objects to reduce the odds of a collision even more."

"And then it's on to Jupiter?"

"Yes, Nellie will head to Jupiter for a huge gravity assist that will project it upward from the Solar Plane toward the asteroid and Moriarty," Jamie replied as she displayed the flight path. "We'll talk about these other details later as the mission progresses, but the assist from Jupiter will occur 123 weeks into the mission."

Jamie was getting ready to leave when she saw a small hand raised from the back of the room. That week, Assawoman was hosting one of its many space programs for children. The small hand came from a group of junior astronauts who were there to experience their first press briefing.

"OK, one more question," Jamie said, pointing to the student astronaut.

"How is Commander Freeman getting along with the robots?" she asked to the laughter of many in the crowd, including Jamie.

"From what I can tell, that's going great," Jamie replied. "LB, the logical robot, has been very helpful carrying out many tasks. RB, the more emotional robot, has surprised us all with his interesting behavior. We think that the robot designer, Frances Kelmar, made a special effort to give RB some personality traits that would keep Commander Freeman on her toes. OK, thank you all for being here. I look forward to the next briefing."

26

SPACE JUNK

The trip from Earth to Mars went smoothly. Because Mars would be the last stop for any repairs, the Control Center had Colleen run systems checks on a daily basis. They also rehearsed procedures for Moriarty and planet C. There was very little down time.

Thirteen weeks into the mission, it was determined that a Mars stop was not needed because Nellie was performing beautifully. The Control Center relayed course corrections to Colleen for a more direct approach to Jupiter. Laser-based communications enabled them to send the huge packet of data from Earth to Mars in just three minutes. After confirming the plan, Colleen fired thrusters briefly to adjust Nellie's path.

"Thrusters fired," Colleen announced.

"Roger that," came the delayed response.

She then reported speed and direction to the

Control Center, thereby confirming a successful procedure. Nellie was now on course for a gravity assist from Mars that would speed the spacecraft into the Asteroid Belt in 26 more weeks.

LB and RB took care of routine procedures during the journey to the Asteroid Belt. Colleen had grown quite comfortable with letting them handle tasks that were relatively simple. Their progress was easily monitored through wireless communications between them and Colleen's display panel. Daily chores were automatically checked off as they were completed. Colleen took advantage of her lighter schedule during this time to study and review recent scientific publications that were regularly transmitted from Earth and loaded to the onboard computer library.

"Approaching the Asteroid Belt," LB reported as Nellie finally neared the leading edge of the 150-million-kilometer thick Belt. It was as wide as the distance from the Sun to Earth.

"Yeeha!" RB said to the annoyance of both Colleen and LB.

"Roger, LB," Colleen said. "Tone it down, RB."

"Yes ma'am," RB said. Colleen rolled her eyes.

"We'll need to navigate in real time through the Belt," Colleen said. "It'll now take us ten to twenty minutes to communicate with Earth, twice that for a back and forth. That won't be quick enough if we need to avoid an asteroid, so we need constant vigilance as we make our pass."

"But, Commander," LB said, "aren't the odds of hitting an object in the Asteroid Belt less than one in a billion?"

"I read that, too," RB said. "I don't think we have anything to worry about."

"LB, you're right about asteroid bodies, but there are also fragments of spacecraft in the Belt now."

"Oh, yes, Commander," LB said. "I know that over a century ago space was militarized by a rogue leader who believed that space was his domain."

"Correct," Colleen said. "He created a special force to control space for his country alone. He was too foolish to understand that others could also create their own space forces, which they did. Within twenty years, there were thousands of military satellites and even a few spacecraft that were weaponized to protect what had been a neutral area of commerce and scientific discovery for all."

"Wasn't there a war on Mars?" RB asked.

"No, not a war," LB said, "but there was an incident. A software problem caused one country's satellite to fire on another, and soon there were many satellites and spacecraft blown up around Mars and Jupiter."

"And the space debris was spread across the half-billion kilometers between the planets, with some settling in the Asteroid Belt, particularly on the inner and outer edges," Colleen said.

"But haven't those fragments been tracked?" RB asked.

"Just around Jupiter and Mars," LB said.

"Still," Colleen said, "the odds of Nellie running into space junk or asteroid bodies is very slim."

"But not zero," LB added.

"Right," Colleen said, "and that's why we need to be vigilant."

"I've initiated the tracking system," LB said.

"Roger, LB," Colleen said. "RB, initialize sensors for tracking unmapped debris."

"I'm on it," RB said. It had become very clear to Colleen that Kelmar had programmed RB to avoid formalities in most circumstances. This didn't bother Colleen because she never really considered herself a commander so much as a scientist. If the mission could support two humans she would have happily yielded to another commander. Her interest was simply to get to planet C and encounter alien life forms. Despite this slight indifference to her supervisory role, however, she still felt obligated to reign in RB to some extent.

"I'm on it, *Commander*," Colleen replied.

"Why?" RB asked. "And I am certainly not the Commander. Why, I couldn't imagine."

"Why what?" Colleen asked before realizing what was going on. "Oh, just refer to me as your Commander, RB. OK?"

"Yes, ma'am," RB replied as LB smacked him on the backside. "Hey!"

"Stop it, LB," Colleen said. "Let's just do our jobs here."

Passage through the Asteroid Belt was not very interesting to Colleen because objects were either so small or far away that they couldn't be observed directly. As they approached the far edge and neared Jupiter, however, things picked up as the crew began planning for the huge gravity assist that would propel them toward the asteroid and Moriarty.

Colleen was quietly reviewing instructions transmitted from Earth when sirens suddenly blared and alerts flashed on her display.

"What in the world?" she said.

"Commander, Commander," LB said, rushing to her side. "Nellie has been hit."

"Hit?" Colleen asked, surprised that the spacecraft could be hit without her feeling a jolt of any sort. "Hit by what?"

"I cannot tell," LB said, "but it looks like an object struck the Barge."

"Yes, I can see that now on my monitor," Colleen said, "but I can't get much information from here."

"Why not?" RB asked, joining them in the cockpit.

"The Barge was added after Nellie was designed and built for the mission to planet C," LB said, "so it isn't fully equipped with sensors and monitors like other parts of Nellie."

"You'll need to go back there and check it out, LB," Colleen said. "RB, send a message to the Control Center. Let them know that the Barge has taken a hit, and LB is going back for an inspection."

"Got it," RB said.

"The only way to access the Barge is by EVA," Colleen said to LB, using the shorthand for extravehicular activities. "You'll have to go out the aft EVA hatch on Hab, tether, and then enter the Barge through its fore EVA hatch." She had pulled up a holographic display of Nellie to indicate the pathway LB would take.

"Roger," LB said. "I've been programmed for EVAs, so am ready to go."

"Do you have 3-D mapping of the Barge in your memory banks?"

"Roger."

"OK, then, let's get started."

LB fired her thrusters to head back through Hab but then turned them off when she realized Colleen could not keep up with her. When they reached the airlock at the back end of Hab, LB prepared for the EVA. Because she was a robot she wouldn't need a helmet or special suit, just a tool pack and the tether. Within minutes she was through the airlock and tethered to Hab for the short spacewalk to the Barge.

"Opening the hatch," LB reported. The Barge had a thin skin and was not pressurized. The FRRs were each held in their own pressurized containers, however, to protect them on the journey. LB quickly examined the hull to see if she could determine if it was penetrated. Within a few minutes she found a small hole in the aft area.

"Commander, I have found a single puncture in the hull."

"Can it be patched?"

"Roger. It should be quite easy to patch."

"Is there any other damage?"

"Not that I can see ... oh, wait," LB said. "I believe I see."

"See what?"

"Commander, I believe I see a hole in one of the FRR containers."

"Can you see any damage to the rocket?"

"I cannot see well enough through the container. Permission to open the container, Commander."

"Permission granted," Colleen replied. "It's already been depressurized because of the hole, so let's have a closer look to see if the rocket itself has been damaged."

The FRR containers were designed to be opened remotely when the rockets were launched. LB accessed her memory banks to determine how to open them manually. It was a fairly simple task that she completed in ten minutes.

"Container removed," LB reported.

"OK, what can you see?" Colleen asked.

"Well, Commander, it looks like the guidance system was hit. I can't tell what hit it and am unable to fully assess the damage."

"There were no mapped asteroid objects in our

path, so I assume it was space junk," Colleen said. "Are you sure it's the guidance system?"

"Ninety-nine percent certain, Commander," LB replied.

"OK, I guess we'll need to operate assuming we now have just five FRRs," Colleen said. "RB, send a message to the Control Center telling them that we need a new plan for the asteroid. We are down to five rockets so need to reassess the landing spot and orientation for each."

"Oh, my, that's not good," RB said. "Not good at all."

"Send the message," Colleen said firmly.

"OK, um, Commander," RB said in a lame attempt at formality.

LB completed her inspection and returned to Hab. As they slowly made their way back to Com, LB and Colleen discussed their plan for developing an approach for landing five rockets on the asteroid.

27

ROCKET PLAN

"Well, that's why we loaded six," Min said.

"But is that really enough?" Jamie asked.

"We have a lot of uncertainty here," Min said. "Asteroid mass, direction, and speed. Moriarty mass, direction, and speed. Suitable landing sites on the asteroid. All educated guesses."

"Yes, we all know that Min," Jamie said. "But, if we successfully land five FRRs, will we be able to accelerate the asteroid enough to budge Moriarty?"

"I think so," Min said.

"And that is what Earth's fate rests upon," Dave said, "your opinion."

"It's more than an opinion, Dave," Min said angrily.

"I didn't mean to offend you, Min," Dave said.

"I'm just frustrated; that's all."

"Understood," Jamie said. "We all are."

"Lebron," Jamie said, turning to the Barge builder, "do you think the FRR launches have been compromised by the damage?"

"I can't see why they would be," Lebron said. "Even the damaged rocket may be launchable."

"But we are unlikely to be able to control it," Min said.

"True," Lebron said, "but we still have some hope. Let's build on that."

"Agreed," Jamie said. "We need to plan for five rockets with the potential for a sixth."

"That's essentially the same as planning for five, isn't it," Dave said.

"Yes," Min said, "except that we may be able to get a partial assist from the sixth to put us over the top."

"That's what I mean," Lebron said. "Don't give up."

"Got it," Jamie said. "Min, you need to take the

lead on this with help from Lebron. Bring in Carla for the mapping side." Min and Lebron nodded in agreement.

"OK, send some details on our strategy to Colleen so she can help us out," Dave said to Jamie.

"We'll send it out later today," Jamie replied.

"We have plenty of time to come up with a plan," Colleen said to the robots.

"That is true, Commander," LB said.

"I'm not feeling good about this," RB said. "What if five FRRs are not enough or we have trouble with one of them? Then what?"

"Don't be so emotional, RB," Colleen said. "LB did a thorough assessment, so I'm convinced that only one rocket was damaged. We don't even know if the damage is too severe to launch it. I'm sure that the Mission Team at the Control Center is considering our options and working on a plan."

"OK, boss, but I'm still worried," RB said.

"I find it increasingly difficult to understand how

the same creator made both of us," LB said. "You are a driveling mess at times, RB."

"Hey, LB, take it easy on him," Colleen said. "I have my doubts as well, but I'm not wired like he is. Nor are you. Now please get back to work assessing landing options for five FRRs using the maps Carla provided."

"Roger, Commander," LB said before heading off to her work area in Hab.

"RB, please go tend the gardens," Colleen said, hoping this would alleviate his concerns.

"OK, but ...," RB began. Sensing Colleen's frustration with him, he stopped talking and hustled back to the gardens he had taken care of just a few hours earlier.

With the robots assigned tasks, Colleen could now focus on her analysis of options for the five remaining rockets. She had yet to find a solution that would provide the thrust needed within acceptable error margins, a problem that troubled her greatly. While confident that the Mission Team could develop a proposal that might work, she felt deep down that everyone was relying on her for the ultimate solution. She thought LB would be of little assistance due to a lack of much needed creativity.

Communications between Colleen and the Control Center were less than candid. The Mission Team didn't want to create doubts in Colleen's mind, and she didn't want to say that the mission was doomed based solely on her own initial analysis. As a result, they all hedged their conclusions and said there was more to do before they could be certain of their options. Despite this, Jamie and Dave were pretty sure that five FRRs would not be enough without a lot of luck. Colleen had reached a similar conclusion.

Min and Lebron, however, were more optimistic, even though their assessment was far from complete. Lebron's influence had caused Min to consider many options for launching and controlling the damaged FRR that he otherwise would have ignored. While evaluating the data, he reminisced about the time when Colleen had corrected several of his mistakes at Northern. That had greatly perturbed him at the time, but it pleased him now given that it had led to a better career path. Min felt deeply indebted to Colleen and wanted to do what he could to guarantee her success on the mission. Helping Colleen save

Earth would, of course, be an amazing accomplishment that nothing else in his career could top. But on a more personal level, Min felt that helping the woman who was instrumental in shaping his career was also important, even if she still seemed to resent him.

Min and Lebron's plan development was complicated by the lack of resolution in Carla's maps. Carla noted that there was no way to improve the maps from Earth. Although Colleen had mapping instruments on Nellie that could be used to refine the maps, round-trip communication time would be just under two hours. The window of opportunity for landing and firing up the FRRs was such that the Control Center would have a chance to send only one, maybe two, sets of instructions after Colleen had collected and transmitted the mapping data to Earth. Still, Min and Lebron planned to lock in tentative locations and launch parameters for both a five- and six-rocket approach, making adjustments on the fly after getting better mapping data from Colleen. Min knew that this plan would fall far short of satisfying Dave, Jamie, and Colleen, but he believed they would all recognize that this was their best option.

"What?" Dave hollered. "Is that the best we can do?"

"Yes, it is, Dave," Min replied.

"If we lock in a plan with all of the uncertainty we have about the asteroid, we will guarantee failure," Lebron added.

"Colleen won't like this," Dave said.

"She'll understand it," Jamie said. "None of us like it, but I think it makes sense."

"I didn't say it didn't make sense," Dave said. "I'm, well, I trust your analysis Min, Lebron. I really do. It's just too much like a wildcard."

"I couldn't agree more, Dave," Min said. "As an engineer, this is not something that generally makes me comfortable. But, it *is* our best option."

"We'll make it work," Lebron added.

"We need to share this with Colleen and have her work with Carla on the mapping approach," Jamie said. "She loves a challenge."

"So true," Dave said. "Thank you all. Let's get this to Colleen ASAP."

"Got it," Jamie said. "We'll get her started on this as we work out the details on the Jupiter gravity assist."

"And make sure to be clear in the briefing that Colleen still needs to review this," Dave said.

"No problem," Jamie replied.

28

DAY 487 – PRESS BRIEFING

"Good morning," Jamie said to the assembled press. "You are probably all aware that the Hab segment of Nellie was hit by space debris a few days ago. The spacecraft had largely completed its seven-month journey through the Asteroid Belt when the incident occurred. Today we'll talk about that and our plans moving forward. I have with me Lebron King, the designer of the Barge, and Dr. Min Ri, designer of the FRRs, or fission reaction rockets."

Jamie cast a map showing where Nellie was when the debris hit, followed by images of the damage on Hab. "As you can see from the images, the space debris blew a small hole in the Barge's thin skin. We believe that one of the FRRs was damaged as well. We've since begun to develop a plan to continue the mission with or without the damaged rocket. I'll hand it over to Mr. King now for a quick discussion of the Barge damage."

Lebron stood and said, "As Dr. Bishop has stated, there is only a thin outer skin on the Barge. In addition, the Barge is not pressurized, a design that has worked out well for us at this point. Each of the FFRs has a separate pressurized container, and only one of those has been damaged. The robot LB navigated back to the Barge, removed the container for the damaged rocket, and assessed the damage. We believe that there is potential harm to the rocket's navigation system, but we can't fully assess the problem. There is, however, a chance that the damaged rocket will still function correctly."

"Why can't you fully assess the problem?"

"Well, the Barge and FFRs were added in a rush after it was determined that Moriarty would indeed impact the Solar System. We had a very short timeframe to design and build these components so had to do away with some of the more advanced features of problem diagnostics and other nice, but not necessary, capabilities."

"Then, your assessment of damage is largely guesswork?"

"No, it's not guesswork, but it's not complete. The robot LB did a fine job determining the damage."

Day 487 - Press Briefing

"And that's why we are working on two plans for the FRRs," Jamie added, jumping in to direct the discussion away from the discussion of problems to that of solutions. "Dr. Ri will now describe those plans for you."

"Yes, um, there are six FRRs on the Barge," Min began, surprised by the sudden segue, "with the sixth being an extra for situations just like this." Jamie was pleased that Min was taking a more positive approach with the press than he had in discussions with the Mission Team. "As Lebron indicated, it is entirely possible that all six FRRs will perform properly, but we are developing two plans, one for all six rockets, and one for just five."

"When will you decide on which plan to use?"

"First, keep in mind that these plans have not been finalized. That said, we'll know if there is a serious problem with the navigation system of the sixth rocket after we launch it from the Barge. If we determine that it cannot land on the asteroid, we will immediately switch to the five-FRR plan."

"Will you use different landing locations for the two plans?"

"No, the landing locations are the same. That's the

A Complicated Journey 181

beauty of our approach. The FRRs can't be relocated after landing, so our plan avoids that problem by using sites that work for both options. After they land, however, we can adjust the directions in which they point. That allows us to make adjustments unique to each option."

After some discussion about the design details of the rockets, Jamie described the mapping component. She noted that Colleen and Carla were still sharing ideas on the best approach.

"How will you share all of that information in such a short period? Will there be enough time to get it all done and launch the rockets on time?"

"That's a great question," Jamie said. "While communication time will be long during mapping, taking about 37 minutes one way, we are able to pack a lot of data into each second of communication."

Jamie then used this opportunity to cast a diagram showing the network of stationary satellites that would be used to send communications between Earth and Nellie. They would transmit infrared laser beams at the speed of light. She noted that nothing could travel faster than the speed of light in a vacuum, another of Albert Einstein's time-

Day 487 - Press Briefing

tested observations. Technology, however, had been developed over the years to carry more data at the same speed.

"OK, last question," Jamie said, pointing to an individual near the back of the room.

"Given that Moriarty is a gas giant, how do you expect to crash an asteroid into it to move it? Won't the asteroid just pass right through Moriarty?"

Jamie controlled her urge to scoff at such an idiotic question, replying, "That's an interesting question. As has been demonstrated for Jupiter, we believe that there is a good chance that Moriarty has a core of metals and rocks. Whether it even has a core or hard surface is immaterial, however. The asteroid will have a gravitational influence on Moriarty, which is what we are counting on to shift the planet's trajectory a tiny bit. The asteroid, of course, will burn up as it passes through the dense atmosphere."

Jamie then quickly adjourned the briefing. She was relieved that the briefing was over and she could get back to the more important work of the mission.

29

DAY 859 – PRESS BRIEFING

"Well, it's been awhile," Jamie said as introduction to the first press briefing she had conducted in months. "I see some new faces in the room. Welcome. Today, I'll bring you up to speed on the latest mission developments. First, you are probably all aware that Nellie has been slowly inching its way toward Jupiter. The spacecraft will finally be close enough to engage in the big gravity assist in three days. Let me give you some more details on this event."

After casting a simulation of the assist, Jamie said, "The journey to planet C requires a gravity assist from both Jupiter and Moriarty. Right now, Nellie is traveling at about eight kilometers per second. That's fast, but not nearly fast enough to get Commander Freeman to C in her lifetime. The Jupiter assist will increase that speed to about 150 kilometers per second, and the Moriarty assist will kick it up to 400 kilometers per second. That is nearly twice the top speed to date for a human spacecraft. You may recall that we achieved that speed on the first mission to orbit Neptune."

"How long will it take Nellie to reach planet C?"

"After Jupiter it'll be another twelve years," Jamie replied. "That's a long way off, so let's focus on the near-term encounter with the asteroid and Moriarty. This, of course, is the primary purpose of the mission."

Jamie now cast a simulation of the mapping procedure, providing additional details as it played out. "As you can see, this will be a very busy period as we lock down the best landing sites for the FRRs before they are launched from the Barge."

"When will this all begin, the mapping I mean?"

"We are still finalizing some details, but Nellie will reach Jupiter in three days, as I've said. It will then take 23 days for the mapping to begin. Because of Nellie's speed, however, we believe that the mapping and launching of the FFRs from the Barge will both need to be completed within a 24-hour period. We will then have about eight hours for FFR landings on the asteroid, orientation of the rockets, and firing of the rockets to begin moving the asteroid toward Moriarty."

"When will you all sleep?"

"Afterward," Jamie said, before adding, "I hope."

30

DOUBLE ASSIST

Colleen had set aside her work on the asteroid after sending her latest mapping recommendations to Carla. While she was deeply committed to carrying out the Moriarty part of the mission, nothing could approach the enthusiasm she had for the journey to C.

Colleen reviewed the plans for the Jupiter gravity assist, updating calculations based on the latest data sent from the Control Center on the paths of Moriarty and the asteroid. Because Nellie would be traveling faster than the asteroid even after the FRRs had fired, Colleen wouldn't know about the success of that effort until after she had passed around Moriarty for the gravity assist. That meant she would be heading to C not knowing if Earthlings would need it some day soon as a place to settle.

Nearly two-and-a-half years into the journey, technicians at the Control Center confirmed

Colleen's latest calculations, and Nellie was cleared for the Jupiter rendezvous. Colleen fired thrusters to adjust Nellie's course in accordance with the updated flight plan. Because signals from Earth to Nellie now took about 33 minutes, Colleen's course adjustments would be completed without real-time communications with Earth. She was on her own.

"Speed and approach angle are now optimal," LB said.

"Roger," Colleen replied.

"Gravitational force is increasing to target level," LB said.

"Roger. All systems are go."

Nellie passed within 250,000 kilometers of Jupiter's cloud tops before surging away toward Moriarty at 150 kilometers per second. Nellie's speed had increased nearly twenty-fold.

"We're on our way now," Colleen said.

"Roger, Commander," LB said.

"RB, are you there?" Colleen asked, surprised at the lack of reaction from the emotional robot.

"Yes, I am," RB said.

"What, no 'yeeha'?" Colleen said.

"No," RB said.

"Why not?" Colleen asked.

"Perhaps he's learned a bit about proper protocol, Commander" LB said.

"I'm nervous about the FRRs. What if the Mission Team can't come up with a plan that works? Will we still go back to Earth knowing it is doomed? What if we continue on our journey and find that we are unwelcome at C? Where do we go then? Where do *you* go, ma'am?" RB said.

"We *will* have a plan that works, RB," Colleen said. "I'm certain of that."

"One cannot be truly certain, Commander," LB said. "There must always be some uncertainty, doubt."

"It's not always about math, LB," Colleen said. "We sometimes need to have a bit of faith, in ourselves and in others." Colleen paused briefly, surprised to hear those words coming from her own mouth.

"Faith has no value, Commander," LB said. "It is intangible."

"Just in," RB interrupted, "a message from the Control Center."

Colleen cast the message so all could see it, even though it wasn't necessary because LB and RB instantly absorbed every message electronically and had both already read it. Colleen simply wanted to use the image as a prop for cheering up RB.

"Looks like they have a plan for landing the rockets," Colleen said.

"Yeeha!" RB said.

"And it relies heavily on the mapping plan you are developing with Dr. Lòpez, Commander," LB said.

"Yes, I'll need to review what she's sent us and send her my final recommendations. Now that we're about done with the mapping plan, let's make sure the equipment is ready," Colleen said. "Run diagnostics on the wide-range scanning laser, LB, so we know it'll be working when we get to the asteroid."

"Roger, Commander," LB said before leaving for Hab to perform the testing.

"RB, do the same for the spectrometer."

"I'm on it," RB said as he chased after LB, the airlock closing behind him.

Colleen then sent a message back to the Mission Team, a communication that would shock Dave while confirming that Jamie was right about her. Colleen told them that she accepted the landing plan as the best alternative and would send Carla final comments on the mapping approach within 24 hours.

31

MESSAGE FROM A FRIEND

"Colleen has developed a perfect plan for mapping the asteroid," Carla said to the group huddled at the Control Center. She was communicating remotely from her office at Hawthorn Tech.

"But the plan gives her only two hours to do the mapping," Dave said. "Will a high-speed flyby give you enough good data?"

"Yes, I believe it can work," Carla said. "She'll take Nellie to within 2,000 kilometers of the asteroid, mapping during the approach. That should give us plenty of data on the side of the asteroid where the landings will occur. Colleen also determined when the mapping needs to begin and end to allow sufficient time to launch the FRRs."

"Right, her plan says that the rockets are launched from Nellie beginning thirty minutes before she reaches her closest approach," Min said. "All launches are to be completed within five minutes."

"So, that puts the first launch at about 270,000 kilometers out," Lebron said.

"Her plan shows that the mapping needs to begin at a distance of 2.3 million and end at about 1.2 million kilometers from the asteroid for there to be time for us to analyze the data and send back recommended landing spots," Carla said. "And to maximize our time, Colleen will be streaming the mapping data as it's collected. It'll take 37 minutes for transmission between Nellie and us."

"But the plan only gives us thirty minutes to analyze the mapping data and pick landing spots to send back to Colleen," Min said. "That's crazy."

"I love it," Lebron said.

"We'll have all five of our supercomputers assigned to the task," Jamie said.

"Colleen will then have less than five minutes to launch the FRRs," Min said, "so we had better be right about the locations."

"Hold on," Dave said. "It'll take the rockets over seven hours to reach and land on the asteroid. That will give you time to communicate with Colleen on their orientation before she embeds them and triggers their thrusters."

"That is correct for the first launch, Dave, but we'll have less than six-and-a-half hours after the last launch" Carla said. "In addition, we'll have less than that time to correct the course of any of the rockets." Dave nodded his agreement.

"OK, she'll then have about six hours after landing to orient the FRRs," Jamie said.

"The rockets will transmit data and images to confirm landing success and help with their orientation," Min said. "We'll need to adjust our orientation plans based on their exact landing positions and attitudes."

"This schedule leaves us about four hours to send final orientation commands to Colleen," Lebron said. "Perhaps we can even squeeze in a nap." Those in the room chuckled at the much-needed infusion of humor.

"Better rest up while you can," Dave said. "As Min indicated, it'll be crazy once we get near the asteroid."

"After the rockets are settled and aimed, Colleen will fire them up remotely from Nellie," Jamie said.

"This is really tight," Dave said. "If anybody has any objections to this plan, let's hear it now." The room was silent.

"OK, I'll transmit the detailed timeline to Colleen," Jamie said.

After a few more back-and-forth communications, Colleen and the Mission Team reached final agreement on the plan. Nellie was only two days into the 23-day journey from Jupiter to the asteroid, leaving plenty of time for Control Center technicians to double-check all plan details. Colleen was busy reviewing the procedures for FRR orientation when she received a private video message from Earth.

"Hi, Colleen, this is Vera. I just wanted to visit with you a bit before the excitement begins."

Vera's message went on to report that she had communicated with Jamie and knew the current status of the mission. She was pleased that most things had gone well and that they had a plan to solve the Moriarty problem with the remaining five rockets. She expressed her confidence in both Colleen and the Mission Team. She then proposed to Colleen that she needed to address her mental health on a regular basis, not waiting for a problem to occur. She was concerned that the pressure and loneliness could take a toll on Colleen if she wasn't proactive in addressing these matters. She asked about the cryogenically-frozen puppy and whether Colleen had considered bringing it back to life.

Radio signals from Earth were now taking close to forty minutes to reach Nellie, creating an unavoidable awkwardness in the communication. It was almost as if they were pen pals, exchanging letters back and forth. Each provided a lengthy reply to the other to increase the efficiency in their communication, but spontaneity was sacrificed.

"I'm very glad to hear from you, Vera," Colleen said. "I've come a long way from Northern, *literally*, but I'm always mindful that this all began in a room with you. A pushy little twelve-year-old argued with a top researcher in the field that she should get to fly in a rocket to a newly discovered planet because some wackos had detected laser signals. Who would have thought that we'd still be on speaking terms, let alone while I'm now in that rocket and on my way?"

Colleen went on to talk about loneliness but denied feeling any. Her interactions with LB, RB, and the Mission Team were enough to meet her needs for socializing. She complimented Frances Kelmar on the design of the robots. She hadn't considered the puppy, other than to be sure LB and RB included it in their routine inspections. She asked Vera about her health, knowing that she was now 69 years old. Colleen had observed in the video message that Vera appeared frail but didn't mention it, another sign that Colleen had matured since her summer at Northern.

Vera said she was feeling great, and after another round of messages they bid farewell. Vera again expressed confidence in the mission's success and wished Colleen the best. Colleen said she wanted to chat again after rounding Moriarty.

Afterward, Colleen entered Hab through the airlock and tended the garden. While she had told Vera she was fine mentally, Colleen took her mentor's message to heart and decided to spend some time relaxing each day. Checking the water lines, she glanced over at the cryogenic chamber. RB had just completed his inspection and was returning to Com to join LB. Colleen walked over to the chamber and observed the sleeping puppy on the monitor.

Cute, she thought.

32

MAPPING

Colleen took advantage of the time remaining before reaching the asteroid by rehearsing the mapping procedures daily with LB and RB. Two hours was a tiny window, and they needed to make the most of every second to get the best data possible for landing the rockets. They also practiced everything from launching the rockets from Nellie to firing them after landing on the asteroid. The steps for landing the rockets on the asteroid would be pre-programmed, but Colleen could intervene if she felt it necessary. The crew was so busy during this period that the mapping date seemed to spring upon them suddenly.

"Well, LB and RB, we're about to start the mapping," Colleen said as they neared their target.

"Ten more minutes, Commander," LB said.

"Take your positions," Colleen said.

"Already there, ma'am," RB said.

"Roger," LB said as she slapped RB on the back of his head.

"Equipment engaged?" Colleen asked.

"Roger," LB and RB said simultaneously, this time with RB revealing his best robot grin. LB responded with a robotic eye roll.

The minutes passed quickly, and the mapping began on schedule. Data transmission to Earth was immediate, with the first packets arriving 37 minutes later. Colleen and the robots wouldn't receive confirmation of successful data transfer until 46 minutes before the mapping was to be completed, too late to adjust the procedure. The Mission Team would have no choice but to use whatever data Nellie sent to them.

Colleen and the robots worked smoothly and rapidly. All mapping was completed as planned. There was no time for celebration, however, because they needed to shift quickly to the FRR launches. Everything that could be done in advance for the launches had already been completed, but they would still need to receive landing targets from the Mission Team and ensure that these targets were successfully programmed into each rocket before launch. This would all have to be completed in less than five minutes.

"Oh captain, my captain," RB said, "can we get this all done on time?"

"Don't worry, RB," Colleen said. "It's under control."

"Yes, you can just watch if you'd like," LB said. "We don't really need you, and it's *Commander* not captain."

"But," RB said.

"*Really*," LB insisted, cutting him off.

"LB, we don't have time for that," Colleen said. "RB, take your place and just do what you've been trained to do. Control your emotions."

"Yes, Captain."

"I'm *not* your captain."

"Right, ma'am." RB ducked as LB tried to swat him.

They all remained in their positions, eagerly awaiting the message from the Control Center.

"What's wrong with that computer?" Min hollered in disgust.

"Relax," Lebron said. "The tech will have it running smoothly very soon, and the other four are working fine."

"We're running out of time," Min said, impatiently.

"Keep your head," Carla said. "The computers are integrated, so the working computers will take over calculations as needed."

"But we may not be able to complete them all in time," Min said.

"Keep an eye on the clock," Carla said. "We can reduce resolution if necessary to ensure that all six landing spots are determined before time is up."

"We'll have six great targets, Min," Lebron said.

"But with greater uncertainty," Min said.

"Yes," Carla said, "but enough certainty for success."

"That's it. Stay positive," Lebron said.

Min wasn't convinced and stalked about the room

as if he was an expectant father. He was a total mess. Carla and Lebron ignored him and stayed focused on the task. Jamie entered the room after being buzzed secretly by Carla.

"How's it going in here?" Jamie asked. "Is everything good, Min?"

"No, one of your computers isn't working," Min said. "Our analysis will be compromised."

"Hey, even if we're off by a little bit, the FRRs will take six to seven hours to reach the asteroid," Jamie said. "We can adjust course while they're in flight, right?"

"Theoretically," Min said, "but communication time is so long now that we'll have limited opportunity to discuss any corrections with Colleen. And she'll want a say in the matter, as you know."

"Let's save that for later, Min," Jamie said. "Right now, I need your coolest head so we can send the landing target instructions to Colleen before it's too late."

"Got it," Min said. His trust in Jamie had never wavered over the years, and she could almost control his emotions at the flip of a switch.

After another ten minutes, they still had only four working computers, so Carla adjusted the program to reduce resolution, thereby speeding up the calculations. With Jamie no longer in the room, Min had begun to lose control again, smacking his hand against a wall and leaving a palm-sized indent.

"Hey, Min," Lebron said, ignoring his outburst. "Get set to send the data packets to Nellie."

Min was responsible for making sure that the data packets were in order before they were transmitted to Colleen. Remembering what Jamie had said, he managed to pull himself together enough to focus on his task.

"Done!" Carla said.

"Send it off," Lebron said.

"I just need a few more seconds," Min said. "There, got it. Everything is on its way."

"Yeah!" Lebron exclaimed.

33

DAY 885 - PRESS BRIEFING

"Today is an important day for us," Jamie said. "Commander Freeman will be launching the six FRRs for landing on the asteroid. If you don't remember, the FRRs are powerful nuclear fission reaction rockets that will be used to push the asteroid into a collision with Moriarty, the rogue planet."

"Is the damaged rocket expected to work?"

"As I noted over a year ago, we don't know if that rocket will work, but we are hopeful. We've developed plans based on either five or six rockets."

"So, the sixth rocket isn't needed? Why didn't you try to fix it?"

"Um, we'd prefer to have all six functioning, of course, but we do believe five can do the job if they are all located and oriented properly before firing. We couldn't repair the damaged rocket because we had neither the necessary diagnostic tools nor replacement parts. You may recall that Lebron King talked about not having time to add diagnostic capabilities when designing and building the barge and rockets."

"Can you guarantee that they will all land successfully on the asteroid?"

"Nothing is guaranteed, but we'll supplement our initial analyses with data collected by Nellie before the launches. I believe that process is underway at this point. The newer data will have greater resolution, allowing a better analysis of where each rocket should land. Keep in mind, however, that the rockets need to work together to move the asteroid from strategically located and coordinated points, so landing options are limited."

"What happens after they land?"

"After landing, Commander Freeman will determine if any adjustments to rocket orientation are needed before the drilling begins. She'll use photos taken by the cameras on each rocket along with other data collected on the landing sites and how the rocket is positioned on the ground."

"Drilling?"

"Yes, each rocket has a huge auger that will bore into the asteroid surface to lock the rocket in place. Embedding the rockets is necessary to prevent misalignment when the thrusters are fired and throttled to full power to move the asteroid."

"My understanding is that this has never been done before, right?"

"Frankly, we are doing a number of new things for this mission, several out of necessity. While spacecraft have used drills to extract samples from various planets and moons for decades, rockets have never used such devices to burrow into the ground. Because Dr. Min Ri had little time for testing new devices, he chose to adapt augers used by asteroid miners. We have full confidence that they will work."

"What if the damaged rocket blows up on the launch pad?"

"Well, we've taken precautions there. The damaged rocket will launch last from the Barge so it can't interfere with the other launches."

"How long will the rockets take to reach the asteroid?"

"That varies. Ironically, the damaged rocket should arrive first. That's because it will ride on Nellie longer. Nellie travels faster than the rockets will go, 150 versus ten kilometers per second. For that reason, each successive rocket has a shorter distance to travel to reach the asteroid. The first rocket will take about seven-and-a-half hours to land, while the last, Number Six, will take about six-and-a-quarter hours."

"How long does it take now to communicate between Nellie and the Control Center?"

"We're at about 37 minutes for one-way communication. That time will actually decrease, however, as Nellie moves past the asteroid toward Moriarty. I believe we'll be at about 25 minutes then."

"So, where will Nellie be when the rockets launch?"

"Let me put up the flight path," Jamie said before casting the three-dimensional map for all to see. "The red line represents Nellie's path, while the green lines show the paths of the rockets. As you can see, Nellie will be past the asteroid before the rockets land. Still, it'll only take about ten seconds for commands to reach the rockets from that distance. The landing sequences are all pre-programmed, so Commander Freeman will not need to send commands for that. She'll have just over six hours between the landing of Number One and firing them all up to move the asteroid. That's a lot to do in a short time, but it's been well rehearsed."

"Why such a rush?"

"We need to begin pushing the asteroid at a specific time so it will collide with Moriarty at the right location," Jamie said. "Even with these powerful rockets and an asteroid fifty miles across, we'll only be shifting the pathway of Moriarty a very tiny bit. It's a huge planet, but a tiny shift played out over hundreds of thousands of kilometers will move it enough to save the Solar System, as can be seen from this animation." With a wave of her hand she changed the holographic display to a simulation of the collision and resulting pathway of Moriarty.

At that point, a staffer motioned to Jamie that it was time to end the press conference.

"OK, I see that it's time to stop now," Jamie said. "I'm needed at the Control Center to monitor the activities underway. I'll be back tomorrow at the same time to report on the rockets. Thank you."

34

ROCKET LAUNCH

"Incoming data," RB said.

Colleen had also seen the message indicator and was already monitoring the transmission to ensure that the target information was delivered correctly to the FRRs. She was uncomfortable knowing there was no time to review the landing targets before launch, but knew that small course adjustments could be made if targeting errors were found later.

"All landing data received by FRRs," Colleen said. "Ready for launch."

"Roger," LB said.

"Initiating launch for rocket Number One," Colleen said.

Launches would be thirty seconds apart, with the damaged rocket last. From the monitor they could all see that Number One launched with no problems. The pressurized container opened before thrusters sent the rocket a few hundred yards above the Barge. Because of their unique mission, the FRRs had thrusters on one end and a large auger on the other end. During flight the auger was encased in a conical cover that also housed landing legs. After rotation to a horizontal position, the main engine was triggered and the FRR headed off to the asteroid. This procedure was repeated three more times with equal success.

After the fifth pressurized container was opened, Colleen sent the command for thruster operation, but nothing happened.

"Oh my," RB said.

"Not now, RB," Colleen said. "LB, check thruster readings."

"Roger," LB said.

LB reported no anomalies so Colleen sent a second command. Nothing.

"I have faith in you, Commander," RB said, much to the annoyance of LB.

Colleen tried again and the thruster lifted the FRR to its launching height for rotation. The main engine worked as expected, and the fifth rocket was on its way.

"We'll need to adjust its speed a bit to make up for the delay," Colleen said.

"Already accomplished," LB said.

"Now for the last one," Colleen said. "Do you still have faith in me, RB?"

"Roger that," RB said with a wink in LB's direction.

LB had already removed the pressurized container during her damage inspection. The thruster performed perfectly in response to Colleen's command, lifting the sixth and final FRR to its launching height.

"Now for the rotation," Colleen said.

"Perfect!" RB said.

"FRR Number Six ready for launch," LB said.

Colleen hesitated before sending the command to fire up the main engine.

"Yeeha!" RB hollered as Number Six began its journey to the asteroid.

"Don't celebrate yet, RB," Colleen said. "It still has over six hours to reach the asteroid. A lot can go wrong."

"Navigation system for Number Six seems to be performing properly," LB said.

"Jettison Barge," Colleen ordered. Lebron's creation had served its purpose and would no longer be of use. Dumping it off would save fuel.

"Roger," LB said. "Barge jettisoned."

"Bye, bye, Barge," RB said, before adding, "Now, that's a load off."

Colleen suppressed a smile to avoid adding to LB's growing annoyance with RB.

Nearly forty minutes later, the Mission Team celebrated the news that all six rockets had launched. Lebron, in particular, was quite happy, hugging everyone in the room. Min, however, was too worried about the navigation system on Number Six to celebrate.

Colleen wasted no time in focusing on the selected landing sites after the rockets launched. It didn't take long for her to see a potential error in the analysis for Number Six, which would be the first to land. She had LB confirm her analysis and then sent a message to the Control Center regarding the error. Carla's reply arrived about two hours later, leaving only four hours before Number Six would land. She agreed with Colleen's assessment and proposed that the Mission Team and Colleen develop independent recommendations for the Number Six landing location. They would then compare results and make a final choice.

"If we hadn't lost that computer there would be no error," Min said.

"Looking back won't help us, Min," Lebron said. "Let's work on solving the current problem."

Carla agreed, and the three ran the data through the computers again to see if an improved landing recommendation would result. Colleen had far less computer capability on Nellie, but she and LB had perhaps better analytic skills than Carla's team. Another two hours passed before the recommendations from the two locations were shared, just two hours before the landings would begin.

Colleen found that the Mission Team's recommendations were not aligned with her own, putting Number Six a few miles from the location she and LB had settled on. With the rocket hurtling toward the asteroid and barely enough time for another back-and-forth with Carla, she decided to make the call and direct the rocket to her preferred landing spot. She recorded the instructions and had LB transmit them to the rocket. Nellie was now a million kilometers beyond the asteroid, and radio signals took four seconds to reach Number Six.

"Redirection confirmed, Commander," LB said after receiving the signal from Number Six.

"Roger," Colleen said. "Now, all we can do is wait and see how the landing plays out. RB, let the Control Center know what we've done."

"Yes, ma'am," RB said. "Message being sent."

During descent, the rockets would eject the protective conical covers from their noses, revealing the auger and landing legs. The telescoping landing legs were designed to adjust automatically to compensate for unevenness in the asteroid surface. Data collected on landing position and orientation would be supplemented with images taken by cameras mounted on each rocket. Colleen would use this information to adjust each rocket's alignment before embedding the devices in the asteroid's surface. The legs would then be collapsed, and the FRRs would burrow into the surface to lock them in place.

Number Six was just over three hours away from the asteroid when Carla and the others saw Colleen's plan for its landing. They quickly checked the calculations, fully aware that there was little they could do about it if she was wrong.

"As expected, she's right," Min said. "We missed a few things that she accounted for."

"I guess you were right as well then," Carla said. "We should have gone with your assessment instead of what Lebron and I had developed."

"Yeah, we're lucky she caught the errors," Lebron said.

"I'll send her a message, Min, saying that you came up with the same spot," Carla said. "She should know that you were on top of it."

"There's no need for that," Min said.

"Even I know she doesn't fully trust you," Lebron said, "and I've had very little time to see the two of you together. Send the message."

"Speaking of messages," Carla said, "did you send the navigation troubleshooting suggestions to her?"

"Yes," Min said. "She should be getting them in a few minutes, but I certainly hope she won't need them. It's a bit of guesswork on my end."

"Number Six navigation malfunction," LB reported. "Running diagnostics."

"Oh no!" RB said, dodging LB's rapidly approaching right hand.

"Got it," Colleen said. "Stabilizing."

Colleen was able to send commands to minimize the degree to which Number Six was steering off course, but did not have full control of the rocket. The allowable margin of error in the flight path was rapidly getting smaller as the rocket neared the asteroid. They needed to get Number Six back on course quickly before the retro rockets fired to reduced its speed.

"Message from the Control Center," RB said.

"Not now," Colleen said.

"It's from Min," RB said before casting the message holographically for all to see.

"Perfect," LB said. "Instructions for handling the navigation system."

Colleen and LB rapidly scanned the message for commands related to the problem they were having.

"There it is," Colleen said. "Let's try that."

LB quickly communicated the selected command sequence to Number Six. RB nervously tapped his metallic fingers while they waited for a positive response from the rocket.

"Anything yet?" RB asked a half minute after LB finished sending the commands.

"Still waiting," Colleen said. "How are the other five doing, LB?"

"All others are right on course, Commander," LB said.

"What about now?" RB asked, his impatience aggravating an already tense situation.

"Quiet, RB," Colleen snapped. "Just ..."

A Complicated Journey

"Commander, Commander," LB said. "I have confirmation now that Number Six is correcting its course."

"Roger," Colleen said. "Let's double check and prepare for the landings."

Only LB could hear the muffled "Yeeha" from RB as he did his best to obey Colleen's directive.

"Well, it looks like Min has saved the day," RB said. "We're lucky he sent those instructions."

"Yeah, you're right," Colleen admitted. "But, we've still got some important steps ahead. Let's stay focused. Remember, the rocket needs to be traveling slowly enough so it can pass around the asteroid a few times before locking in and hovering over the landing spot. Then, the retro rockets will control the final descent. There's a lot that can still go wrong."

35

MORE PROBLEMS

"Number Six has touched down, Commander," LB said.

"Roger," Colleen said. "Number One will land in seventy more minutes. Get started on the landing analysis for Number Six."

"Roger," LB said.

"Imagery is coming in already," RB said. "Camera is performing well."

LB began her examination of the landing site and orientation of Number Six while Colleen monitored the progress of the other five rockets. The crew on Nellie had a lot of work to do in the eight hours before firing up the rockets. While they could not be moved after landing, the direction in which each rocket would point when bored into the asteroid surface would be adjusted in concert with that of the others for maximum thrust and optimal trajectory. Final adjustments would have to wait until after the last rocket landed, six hours and fifty minutes before they would all be fired up.

As each subsequent landing occurred, RB confirmed that the cameras were working and relayed captured images to LB. The images and related data were used by LB to assess the direction in which each rocket was pointing and whether it had a stable landing position. Colleen then reviewed LB's analyses and compared the landing results with what was planned. Any differences between the actual and planned landing locations would need to be considered when deciding how to point the rockets before drilling into the asteroid surface.

The Mission Team had simulated numerous landing scenarios and provided recommendations for pointing the rockets under each scenario. These computer simulations covered a wide range of possibilities, including using either five or six rockets, and location deviances of several hundred meters. They had insufficient time, however, to develop equations that could be applied to landing locations not included in their simulations. Ideally, Colleen would find that the actual landings matched one of the scenarios. In that case, she would just follow the recommendations for pointing the rockets. The likelihood that such a match would occur, however, was very small. Therefore, Colleen would need to find the closest match and then adjust how the rockets should be pointed based on her own analysis. Colleen didn't have the capabilities on Nellie to run additional computer simulations using the actual landing information, so she would need to take advantage of her special ability to assess complex data sets in her head. Although hoping for a match with one of the scenarios, she was ready for the challenge if no match was found.

"Commander, we have a problem," LB said.

"Let me guess," Colleen said. "Number Six?"

"Well, yes, Commander," LB said, "but that's not all. Number Five is also off target."

Colleen quickly examined the data provided by LB. She was emotionless as her mind raced to understand what it meant.

"OK, so Number Six is off by five kilometers, beyond the range used in the simulations. Number Five, however, is within that range."

"Roger, Commander," LB said as RB looked on quietly. Frances Kelmar had clearly programmed RB to know when to be professional.

"Alright, I can handle this," Colleen said. "LB, send this information to the Control Center so they can take a look at it as well. I don't think they will have time to come up with a solution, but let's give them a chance."

"Roger, already done, Commander," LB said. It was protocol to send the data to Earth as soon as possible.

"What can we do to help?" RB asked.

"Double check the data to make sure everything is correct," Colleen said. "Then, I'll need you two to check my calculations."

With that, Colleen waved them off and assessed her options. While the current situation was not envisioned in the planning scenarios, she was able to explore options in her head using the actual locations of Number Five and Number Six.

"Got it," Colleen said after thirty minutes. "LB, run these launch angles and thrust values and see what you come up with. RB, have you checked the data?"

"Yes, Commander," RB said, causing LB to raise an eyebrow. "Everything checks out."

"Great," Colleen said. "Now, help LB with her analysis and get back to me as soon as possible."

RB hustled off to sit next to LB who had gone to her charging chair in Hab. She wanted to be sure that she had full power for the analysis. While the robots could hold a charge for several days, there were multiple locations on the spacecraft for cordless recharging while they were active. They could also sit in designated charging chairs for a quicker boost.

Immediately after receiving the landing data and images from Nellie, Carla and Min led an effort to determine the best option for launch orientation and thrust. There were just over six hours to go before the rockets would be fired, but Min expected that it would take at least four hours for the augers to do their jobs. So, they really had time for just one back-and-forth communication with Colleen before the launch process was set in motion.

Dave and Jamie stepped into the room together, a

sign that the process had just become more complicated. He generally left things up to Jamie in deference to her role as the Mission Manager.

"Hi, Carla, Min," Dave said as he walked over to a meeting table. "Take a seat please."

Carla and Min exchanged quick glances with each other and Jamie before sitting.

"I'm sorry to interrupt at this time because I know you're busy racing against the clock," Dave said. "But, this is about that race. We can't have Colleen make a unilateral decision on this one. It's way too important for it to be placed on one person's shoulders, regardless of Colleen's capabilities. For that reason, Jamie has already sent a message to Colleen informing her that she cannot finalize rocket orientation and trigger the augers without our approval."

"OK, Dave," Carla said, before adding, "You know that we have only two hours to decide, right?"

"And that it takes an hour and fifteen minutes for one back and forth," Min added.

"Yes, I'm fully aware of that," Dave said. "We

need to get it right the first time and hope that she comes up with the same or equivalent approach."

"But, we won't know if they are equivalent without performing an assessment," Carla said. "And we won't have much time for that."

"Which is why we may need to squeeze into the four-hour window you've recommended for the augers, Min," Jamie said.

"We're already hard pressed as it is, Jamie," Min protested. "We've never embedded a rocket before and don't know much about the composition of the asteroid. Drilling could take longer than we estimated. Then what?"

"Then we launch later and throttle up the engines more," Dave said.

"That will only be possible if we have all six," Min said. "With five, they'll already be at full throttle."

"I didn't say it would be easy," Dave said.

Min began to protest, but Jamie stared him down. She knew they didn't have time to argue.

"Is that all?" Carla asked.

"Yes, that's it," Dave replied.

"Let's get back to work," Min said with an eye on Jamie.

Jamie nodded her approval before asking, "Is there anything we can do for you that will help?"

"Yes," Min said. "Make sure all of the computers are working. These simulations are computer hungry."

"Got it," Jamie replied before exiting the room.

───◆─◆─◆───

"Message from the Control Center," RB reported.

"Wow, they were quicker than I expected," Colleen said.

"No, Commander, it's not about the orientation," LB said.

"It's a directive," RB added.

"Really? Really?" Colleen hollered. "A power play? Is that how Dave spends his time now?"

"Well, ma'am," RB said, "maybe he's just trying to

help, you know?"

"No, this isn't helpful," Colleen replied angrily. "We can solve the problem better here, and he knows it."

"Perhaps we should just send your recommendations and hope they concur," RB said, hoping to calm her down.

"Yes, Commander," LB added. "We've completed our analysis and agree with your recommendations."

Colleen, still angry, pulled herself together enough to send the recommendations with a curt message to Jamie. She immediately regretted the tone of her message but couldn't reel it back in.

Carla and Min had nearly completed their analysis when Colleen's recommendations arrived. There were now less than five hours to go before the rockets would be fired up on the asteroid. Even worse, however, to ensure that the augers started on time, they needed to finish their analysis and compare it with Colleen's in just fifteen minutes.

"Look, Carla," Min said. "We're not done yet, and we only have fifteen minutes."

"What are you saying?" Carla asked, knowing the answer.

"I'm saying we need to give the augers a full four hours to do their job."

"OK, so let's just check her plan and scrap ours," Carla said.

"Perfect!" Min said. "But we can't ..."

"I know," Carla interrupted. She knew that Jamie and Dave wouldn't approve of this approach, so they wouldn't tell them about it.

After several minutes of separately plugging the numbers, Carla and Min agreed that Colleen's plan made sense. They messaged Jamie and Dave, who hurried over to meet with them again.

"So, what did you come up with?" Dave asked. "Did you agree with Colleen?"

"We have the same plan," Carla said, carefully selecting her words to avoid an outright lie. She cast an image of the plan, showing the landing locations and launch angles for each rocket.

"You actually got the same results?" Jamie asked. Although somewhat annoyed by the tone of

Colleen's message, she had decided to let it go.

"There are no other results," Min replied. "We have plans for both a five- and six-rocket boost."

"Excellent," Dave replied. "Let her know ASAP, and let's get moving."

Min and Carla nodded and smiled as Dave left the office. Jamie, however, stuck around and looked Min in the eye. Min looked away uncomfortably. He could sense that she suspected that they had simply agreed with Colleen's recommendation, but she didn't say a word. At this point it didn't matter, and they all knew it.

"Message from the Control Center," RB announced unnecessarily. Colleen and the two robots had nothing to do at this point but wait for the response from the Control Center, so they all saw the message as it came in.

"OK, let's make the adjustments to aim these rockets according to our plan," Colleen said. "LB, you've got the first two, RB the next two. I'll take Number Five and Number Six." There was no time to gloat.

"Roger," LB and RB said in unison. "We're on it, Commander." Although LB could sense a small victory in having RB communicate properly with Colleen, she was also a bit unnerved by no longer being able to predict his behavior.

"Number One and Number Two are a go," LB said. Neither required much adjustment.

"Same for Number Three and Number Four," RB said immediately after LB's report.

"Number Five is good as well," Colleen reported. "Number Six is …"

"Yes, Commander?" LB asked after Colleen dropped off. "Number Six is what?"

"Number Six is lost," Colleen said.

"Lost?" RB asked. "How?"

"It appears to have fallen over," Colleen replied. LB and RB quickly checked the monitors and could tell from the camera image that the rocket had tumbled over.

"I can see a damaged landing leg," LB said. "Look," she added after casting the image.

"I guess it was more damaged by the space junk than we thought," Colleen said before collecting herself. She knew they had only a few minutes before the drilling had to start. "We're down to five rockets, so let's quickly readjust for that plan. Hurry now, but get it right."

LB and RB quickly tweaked the first four FRRs while Colleen adjusted Number Five. After confirmation that all were set, Colleen gave the order to start the augers. She then sent a message to the Mission Team.

"We're down to about three-and-a-quarter hours before launch," Jamie said, seated across from Dave in his office.

"Everything OK?" Dave asked.

"Well, we're also down to five rockets," Jamie replied.

"What happened?" Dave asked as Carla and Min joined them.

"A leg snapped off Number Six," Min said.

"Space junk damage," Jamie added.

"Darn, what next?" Dave said, his frustration boiling up.

"You never said it would be easy," Jamie reminded, hoping to elicit a smile from Dave. It worked. They all laughed despite the difficulty, but Min's laugh was somewhat forced. Now his rockets really had to work as designed or the whole mission would fail.

"She has a five plan, right?" Dave asked just to be sure.

"Yes, and it's the only plan for five," Carla replied, once again choosing her words carefully.

"I assume that the augers have already been drilling for the better part of an hour," Jamie said.

"OK, I guess we just sit back and wait for word from Colleen," Dave said.

"That's all we can do," Jamie agreed. "Carla, you and Min need to take a break. You've been grinding for hours on this. Get some dinner or something and come back in three hours, alright?"

Carla and Min thanked Jamie and left the room. Carla chose to take a nap and fell asleep quickly, but Min couldn't sleep, worried both about the performance of the augers and whether the rockets had sufficient power to do their job. As he lay down on a cot in the office, however, his need for sleep eventually overcame his racing mind, and he dozed off.

36

DESTINATION MORIARTY

"Drilling is completed for all but Number Three," LB reported.

"Very good," Colleen said. "We've got another fifteen minutes before launch time."

"The auger for Number Three appears to be stuck, Commander," RB said.

"Have you run the procedures specified for this sort of problem?" Colleen asked.

"Yes, we've reversed the auger multiple times and adjusted the spin rate to see what we could do," RB replied.

"And?"

"And nothing worked," RB said.

"How far in is it?" Colleen asked.

"Half way," RB said.

"Throttle it up," Colleen directed.

"I've given it all she's got, Captain. I can't give her no more," RB said, paraphrasing a line from Chief Engineer Montgomery Scott of the U.S.S. Enterprise. Besides devoting herself to creating some of the world's most advanced robots, Frances Kelmar also seemed to have spent far too much time watching television broadcasts from a century earlier.

"Pardon me, RB," Colleen said, "but what was that all about?"

"Sorry, ma'am," RB replied sheepishly. "I've throttled the auger as far as I can. It doesn't help."

"Keep trying until we launch," Colleen said, knowing that this additional problem could be the last straw. She was already down to the minimum of five rockets, and if one of them didn't perform properly, the asteroid could move too slowly, move in the wrong direction, or both. In each case, the collision with Moriarty would either not happen or occur off target, dooming the mission. She instructed LB to do what she could to help RB solve the problem.

LB quickly reviewed everything that RB had

attempted and then added a new twist. Min had selected augers that could also be used in a hammer mode, so LB directed RB to give that a try. After several iterations, the drill broke through the difficult material and inched farther toward the penetration goal. Too much time had passed, however, to enable them to get beyond seventy percent of the target.

"Seventy percent will have to do," Colleen said. "Good work, LB." She could see that RB's shoulders slumped a bit, so added, "and RB."

"OK, let's fire them up," Colleen commanded. "This is the big test."

"Roger, Commander," LB said. She then sent the command for each rocket to fire its engines, a command received 26 seconds later. Nearly a minute thereafter, RB reported that all had fired as expected.

Thrust would be applied incrementally to minimize the chance that the FRRs would spring free from their moorings. Nellie, hurtling rapidly on its way to Moriarty, was now 7.7 million kilometers away from the asteroid. The time for one-way communication with the rockets was increasing steadily, but communication was no longer important as there was nothing that Colleen could do now to affect the outcome. She had completed the task for Moriarty and could now only wait for the outcome.

Carla jostled Min to awaken him for the meeting with Jamie and Dave. He was in a deep sleep, and Carla had to nearly push him off the cot to get his attention. She won the battle, however, and they joined the two managers just as the message arrived from Colleen confirming that the FRRs had all fired. Min was relieved, but still agonized over whether the thrust would be sufficient to guide the asteroid to a successful collision with Moriarty. It was too early to tell.

"We've done what we can for this part of the mission," Dave said. "Thanks to everyone for all of your efforts."

"So far, everything is within parameters," Jamie added. "That's a remarkable accomplishment given the challenges we've faced in such a short timeframe."

"What do we do now?" Carla asked.

"We wait to see what happens to the asteroid, and we turn our attention to the mission to planet C," Jamie replied.

Just then a message appeared on Dave's monitor, a message he cast for all to see.

"It's from SUP," Dave said.

"Really?" Jamie said. "Don't they get enough attention now?"

"You still don't believe in them, do you?" Min said, referring to the conversation that Jamie had had years ago with Colleen. Jamie hadn't mentioned it to him, but he heard about it from colleagues who knew Colleen before she had learned about discretion.

"These signals must be real," Carla observed. "I see no reason to doubt that, but what do they mean?"

"Well, SUP seems to think that they are simply looking for friends in the universe," Dave replied.

"They must have an agenda," Min said. "Wouldn't you have a more serious plan if you spent that much time and resources on sending signals?"

"You may not be aware of our efforts in the 1900s, Min," Jamie said. "We were simply looking for a response back then. Maybe, whatever species that lives on C is doing the same thing. Or, maybe, it's something that can be explained by something other than intelligent life."

"Ever the doubter," Dave said. "I think it's real, but I don't think it's something we should worry about now. I'd rather have Nellie return to Earth and save our resources so we can send another spacecraft to Moriarty if this mission fails."

"There wouldn't be time for that," Jamie said. "Besides, if we fail to stop Moriarty we may need another planet to inhabit. Perhaps C will be just right for that."

"We'd better send this message to Colleen," Carla said. "She'll have a fit if she doesn't get it."

"Yeah, right," Jamie said. "C is her primary interest on this mission. Let's not forget that."

"She won't let you," Dave chuckled. "OK, I'm off for some sleep. Send the message, Jamie, and get some sleep yourself. Another press conference tomorrow?"

"Yep, nearly every day," Jamie said. "It gets tiresome."

37

DAY 886 – PRESS BRIEFING

Refreshed from her long night's sleep, Jamie charged into the auditorium prepared to talk about the previous day's events on Nellie. Instead, she was immediately asked about the signals from planet C.

"Yes, we are monitoring reports on signals from C," Jamie said. "And, no, we are still not sure what they mean."

"Doesn't it prove that there is intelligent life on the planet?"

"While some may argue that, we are a bit more cautious in our assessment."

She fended off several more questions about planet C before turning the focus back on Moriarty.

"As you may recall, the six FRRs, or rockets, were to be launched yesterday from the Barge attached to Nellie. All six were launched successfully and landed on the asteroid. We had a failure later with Number Six, however, when aiming it prior to drilling."

"So, what does that mean?"

"It means we now have just five rockets, but our analyses show that should be enough to achieve our goal of crashing the asteroid into Moriarty, the rogue planet."

"But wouldn't you need to move the rockets to provide the direction and thrust needed with just five compared to six rockets?"

"Great question. I can see you've done your homework on this. As I noted in a previous briefing, we planned the landing locations so they could work with either five or six rockets, knowing that we couldn't move the rockets after they land. We can, however, adjust the aim of the rockets based on where they landed and the number of rockets firing."

"What was the failure with Number Six?"

"You may remember that the Barge was hit by space junk on its way to Jupiter. We believe that, in addition to affecting the navigation system for

Number Six, it also damaged a landing leg. That leg snapped off when Dr. Freeman sent the commands for adjusting its aim. It toppled over."

Jamie then provided information on the back and forth between Colleen and the Mission Team on final adjustments before drilling. She zipped through a discussion of last-minute adjustments made after Number Six failed, and purposely didn't mention the problem with drilling for Number Three. She saw no reason to introduce additional fear and uncertainty regarding the mission. She and Dave had agreed to give honest answers to any questions asked, while at the same time not volunteering information that they thought would trigger alarms unnecessarily.

"At this point in time, the asteroid is moving toward the target at our planned speed of just over ten kilometers per second. At that speed, you could fly from New York City to Honolulu in just over thirteen minutes. It will take the asteroid 173 days to crash into Moriarty."

"Where is Nellie?"

Jamie cast the flight path map again for illustration. "As you can see here, Nellie was nearly eight million kilometers from the asteroid when the rockets were fired. Traveling at 150 kilometers per second, it's about fourteen million kilometers from the asteroid now."

"How will Commander Freeman communicate with the rockets? Isn't Nellie too far away?"

"There is really nothing that can be done now from either Nellie or here at the Control Center. The die is cast. That said, we will be tracking movement of the asteroid from here and providing updates to Commander Freeman. She will now be focused on the gravity assist from Moriarty for the journey to planet C. We'll talk about that in the coming days. Thank you."

Jamie left the room despite many hands waving for additional questions. After giving several press briefings over the past few years, she had learned to control the narrative and not let the story get ahead of her. There would be plenty of opportunity to talk more about the asteroid and Moriarty, but not today. She headed back to the Control Center to check on mission status.

38

DEBRIS

There were 49 days between the firing of the rockets on the asteroid and Nellie's rendezvous with Moriarty. Colleen now had plenty of time to reflect on both the mission so far and what was to come. Even after the gravity assist from Moriarty, it would take nearly twelve more years to reach C.

During the planning stages for the operation, the Mission Team had encouraged Colleen to take advantage of the cryo chamber when she reached this stage of the journey. They said it would prevent her from suffering through the boredom of being alone so long in a desolate region of space. Colleen had limited scientific equipment on board Nellie, so she wouldn't be able to collect much data, particularly from great distances. Still, she could be the first person to observe the outer planets of the Solar System from above, at distances far shorter than those from Earth, and she would also have opportunities to view other celestial bodies from unique vantage points. But, could these observations keep Colleen occupied and content while alone over a span of a dozen years? Would communication with the robots keep her sane, or would she need human interaction?

By the time the asteroid hit Moriarty, it would take nearly four hours for radio signals to reach Earth, and it would take nearly six days when Nellie reached C. Communicating with Jamie, Vera, or others on Earth would become a glorified version of letter writing, a form of communication that had largely been phased out in the past half century. Sure, Colleen and the Mission Team could exchange video messages, but even they would be linear, not similar at all to the normal, spontaneous conversations people would have when in each other's presence.

Despite the suggestions of multiple psychiatrists, as well as Jamie and Vera, Colleen had decided not to use the cryo chamber. Although they had suggested Colleen could choose whatever duration she wanted in the chamber, allowing time awake both at the beginning and end of the journey from Moriarty to C, Colleen argued that cryo chambers had never been used on humans in a space flight of this duration. In her mind, they were not a proven technology. That was a hard argument to dismiss, particularly given that the cryo technology had been routinely applied to humans on Earth for only the past twenty years. The success rate was high for periods of ten to twenty years, but it was not foolproof. For these and other reasons, Colleen had determined she would not freeze her way through the trip to planet C.

"What did you say?" Dave asked Carla.

"Moriarty has what appears to be a huge debris field surrounding it. My colleagues at Hawthorn just told me about it."

"That could be a problem for Colleen."

"That's exactly why the first thing I did after learning about it was to contact you."

"We need to see their data as soon as possible so we can determine what our options are."

"Agreed. I've already asked them to share it, and we'll have it soon. There's another team in Germany that's also been involved with this, and they'll cooperate with us, too."

"Great; thanks. I'll set up a meeting with Jamie tomorrow so we can talk. Is that too soon?"

"Not at all. I'm looking forward to it."

"Wouldn't you like to see this little fella running around the spacecraft, LB?" RB asked while the two robots maintained the puppy's cryo chamber.

"No, frankly, I would not," LB replied. "Who would clean up after it? And what is the purpose of having a four-legged creature running around a spacecraft?"

"You're no fun at all, are you?"

"No, I'm not," LB said.

"Hmm, well I think Colleen would like it," RB insisted.

"Commander Freeman," LB said.

"Like I said," RB replied.

They finished their work at the cryo chamber and moved on to tend to the garden, which was doing very well. Colleen had learned to appreciate the many fresh foods grown on board to supplement the more mundane prepared foods. She had even begun to exercise more frequently since launching the FRRs, using the treadmill and other equipment on a daily basis. For the first time since leaving Earth orbit, it seemed like they had a routine on Nellie.

39

MORE ADJUSTMENTS

"So, what's the bottom line, Carla?" Dave asked. He had asked Jamie and Qadira to join them.

"It's unusual because there isn't a set of rings centered on the equator like we see for Saturn," Carla said, as she cast an image of Moriarty surrounded by what appeared to be a fine haze. "That's probably why we didn't notice it until recently. It's too dispersed. It looks more like a cloud of debris circling the entire planet."

"What is the source of the debris?" Jamie asked.

"We're not sure, but we suspect that Moriarty may have passed near a field of asteroids similar to our own Asteroid Belt, picking up many of the objects along the way."

"What are our options now for circling Moriarty for the gravity assist, Jamie?" Dave asked. "Are we able to avoid the debris?"

"We're looking at several different approaches to see which ones will have the clearest space," Jamie replied. "As you know, we need to ensure that we get enough of an assist to meet our timeline. With a full assist, Colleen will be 48 years old when she reaches C, and at least 63 years old when she returns home. If we go with an approach that gives us only half of an assist, she'll be 60 years old when she reaches C."

"And at least 75 years old when she returns," Dave added. "That's pushing her beyond expectations, more than 41 years in space."

After a brief moment of collective silence, Dave asked, "OK, what can we tolerate in terms of a slowdown?"

"Well, if we only get seventy percent of the planned assist, we'll add five years to the journey out to C," Jamie replied. "Colleen would be 53 years old then."

"And 68 when she returns," Carla added.

"Just among us in the room," Dave said, "we still haven't mapped out all of the details for the trip back. Colleen knows this. We won't have a giant body like Moriarty for a return assist, so it very well could take up to twenty years for her to return."

"That's if she even wants to," Jamie said.

"Right," Dave said. "But, we need to assume she's coming back. Let's go with seventy percent as the minimum assist and see what we can do."

"I think we're overlooking spacecraft speed," Qadira cautioned. "Nellie will be ramping up to 400 kilometers per second during the assist. That's fifty times the speed it had when the Barge was struck by debris. I'm not sure Nellie will be able to endure multiple hits at that speed."

"Yeah, there's that, too," Dave lamented. "Does anybody have good news?"

They all chuckled lightly and shook their heads. Dave had his ups and downs as a leader, but he was usually good at recognizing when a bit of humor was needed. All Mission Team members would refer to themselves as optimists if asked, but even they could become frustrated at times.

After a wide-ranging discussion, it was agreed that they needed to go with a minimum seventy-percent assist despite the risk of damage to Nellie.

While the density of debris in Moriarty's cloud was not yet known, an assumption of density similar to that found in the Asteroid Belt would indicate a low probability of collisions. In addition, because Nellie's approach to Moriarty would bring it closer to Earth, there remained a possibility for using the assist to send the spacecraft home if necessary.

"I think it's time to tell Colleen," Dave said after they reached agreement on a plan.

"I'll send her a message," Jamie offered. "She may be able to use her mapping instruments to gather more information on the cloud, and we all know she'll want to confirm any calculations we make on the flightpath and resulting assist."

"I'll make sure the contingency plans are in good shape if Nellie encounters debris," Qadira said.

"My team will continue working with others to get more data on the cloud," Carla said. "I've heard that several other scientific missions have redirected their instruments and analysts to Moriarty to help out. There are a couple of probes around Venus that may be helpful."

"All good," Dave said. "Thanks, everyone. We'll

need to talk more frequently now to stay on top of this. Carla, can you stay in town for another week or two, or do you need to go back to Hawthorn?"

"I can work from here. Jamie has given me a nice work station."

"Great. Although we haven't discussed it, I'm sure you're all aware that the debris cloud could also interfere with the asteroid when it nears Moriarty. Carla, could you also look into the odds of us having a problem with the collision?"

"I'm on it," said Carla.

Immediately after receiving the message from Jamie, Colleen began an analysis of options for the assist. She, too, considered her age when reaching C, concluding that a five-year delay wouldn't be a big deal in terms of her physical condition. However, the delay still bothered her because the mission was already so long. Her response indicated a preference for assuming greater risk with a shorter flight duration, but she knew that Jamie and Dave could not defend that sort of approach publicly.

40

DAY 892 – PRESS BRIEFING

"Good afternoon," Jamie said to the gathered members of the press. "I didn't expect to be seeing you again so soon, but we've had another important discovery since our last briefing."

Their interest already piqued by the surprise announcement of another briefing, the reporters in attendance immediately raised their hands and peppered Jamie with questions from their seats. Now a seasoned veteran of these gatherings, Jamie raised her hands to calm them down, refusing to answer any questions before she gave her presentation.

"OK," she said. "I see you have a lot of questions, but I'll hold off on answering them until after I provide my update."

Jamie was alone for this presentation, not wanting to put either Carla or Qadira on the spot to respond to questions for which they had no clear answers. Their time was better spent working on the answers. She cast an image of Moriarty after the crowd settled down.

"From what I know, none of this information has been leaked," Jamie said, "so this should be new to all of you. Here we have Moriarty as we knew it a few days ago, a very large but simple planet."

As the image morphed into a current depiction with the debris cloud, she said, "And here is Moriarty as we know it today. You can see there is now a cloud of objects surrounding the planet. We're not sure of the origin of the cloud but believe it may have resulted from Moriarty passing through something similar to our own Asteroid Belt. Please keep in mind that Moriarty is a rogue planet, the orbit of which we've seen only a small part. Regardless of its source, the debris cloud presents challenges for us as we try to navigate Nellie around Moriarty for a gravity assist."

She then cast a simulation showing various flightpaths and the resulting percentage assist that each path would generate. "The green line here shows the original path planned for the gravity assist. As you can see, there is considerable interaction with the debris cloud as we understand it today. As we move to smaller gravity assists by swinging wider around Moriarty, we have a lower probability that Nellie will strike an object in the cloud. The time it will take to reach planet C increases, however, because Nellie will be traveling at a slower pace. Our current challenge is to select a flightpath that minimizes the risk of collisions while maximizing the gravity assist. We are working on that now."

"Does Commander Freeman know about this, and what does she think if she does?"

"Yes, we are in full communication with Dr. Freeman, and she is helping us with the analyses. Just like us, she sees it as a challenge. We expected many challenges on this mission, and we are all prepared to deal with them."

"What happens if Nellie is hit by debris? The spacecraft is going really fast now, right?"

"That's a good question. Our engineers are working with Qadira Nagi to address that concern and make sure that the contingency plans are solid. As far as the potential extent of damage, well, that depends on the size of the object and where on the spacecraft it would hit. Beyond that, I can't really answer your question."

"But, didn't you lose one of the rockets because the Barge was hit? It passed right through it, right?"

"Yes, it passed through, but the Barge was a very thin-skinned vehicle. All other parts of the spacecraft, particularly Com, where the Commander sits, have much better protection."

"What about the asteroid? Will it be blown apart if it hits debris?"

"We are working on that question as well. Initial analyses indicate that the odds are small that the debris will shatter the asteroid. There is nothing we can do about it now, so we just need to hope for the best."

Several other questioners described other doom scenarios, and Jamie batted them all back with non-answers. Her objective was to convince the press and its followers that they shouldn't be too concerned because the Mission Team was on top of the problem. She wasn't sure she succeeded.

41

ODDS AND PERCENTAGES

"That thing is huge," RB exclaimed as he observed Moriarty from Com. "It fills the sky." Each of the robots had special capabilities to see dim objects in the darkness of space, while Colleen relied on the specially-equipped monitor in Com to provide an enhanced view for greater visibility.

"And we're still three days away," Colleen said.

"The debris cloud extends farther out than we thought, Commander," LB said. "I just saw a few objects on the monitors." They used monitors because they were traveling so fast that even the robots couldn't directly observe the objects passing by.

"Roger," Colleen said, her voice wavering slightly. "We'll just have to hope we're lucky. Our course is locked in for the assist. We've got our contingency plans, and we're all ready, right?"

"You seem a bit nervous, ma'am," RB said. "We'll

be fine."

"No, RB, I'm not nervous," Colleen lied. "I'm just focused on the situation, as you should be as well."

RB knew he was right. Colleen *was* worried, but he couldn't do anything about it. He was programmed to recognize that this was not a time for levity, so simply bowed to the situation. "Roger, Commander."

"This isn't what we'd hoped for, Dave," Carla said as the group gathered for another session. "Every indication we have from our sources is that the density of the cloud is at least 1,000 times that of the Asteroid Belt. To top it off, the cloud extends farther out than we expected."

"Into our seventy-percent flightpath?" Dave asked, worried.

"Yes, but we've always expected some interaction with the debris cloud on that path," Jamie said.

"Well, the cloud is less dense on the outer edge, but it's still probably a hundred times denser than the Belt," Carla added.

"So, what are the odds of a strike?" Dave asked, fully aware that any estimate would be a fairly wild guess.

"I wouldn't worry about that, Dave," Carla said.

"I'm not worried," Dave said, looking around, "any more than the rest of you. What are the odds?"

"Our best guess is one in ten thousand," Carla replied. "But, we could be way off."

After a few moments of silence, Jamie said, "We're not going to tell Colleen about that."

"She already knows," Qadira said, casting a new message from Nellie, "and they've already detected a few objects."

"Jamie, have you had any luck getting Vera to come here?" Dave asked.

"Yes, she should be here later today. She got our message and said she's more than willing to help."

"Good," Dave said. "I guess that's all we can do for now. Thanks everyone."

―◆― ―◆― ―◆―

"Whoa! That was close," RB exclaimed. "We just had two more objects pass by, one the closest yet."

Both RB and LB were now viewing the monitors to track debris. The frequency of near-misses was increasing.

"Perhaps that was the worst of it, Commander," RB added, trying to keep Colleen from worrying too much. He didn't need to bother with that, however, because she was too busy monitoring conditions to think about the risk. Everything was happening at lightning speed now.

Suddenly, Nellie began to roll wildly out of control. Colleen was smashed against Com's wall and RB and LB were ejected from their seats. LB was the first to rise, and immediately assessed the situation. Colleen was injured, but alert.

"Commander," LB reported, "it appears that we've been hit." LB secured herself to her seat to avoid being ejected again. RB, meanwhile, had made it back on his feet and was assisting Colleen.

"Where? Where were we hit?" Colleen asked, as RB helped the Commander pull herself into her seat. She was already dizzy from the rolling.

"Hab, Commander," LB reported. "Hab has lost pressure."

"OK, RB, assess the damage on Hab," Colleen ordered. "LB, help me stabilize the spacecraft. We've got to get out of this spin."

Colleen passed out from dizziness after giving the commands. RB hustled through the airlock to Hab and LB made sure Colleen was secure in her seat before taking over the controls to stabilize Nellie. In a few minutes LB was able to end the rolling and immediately checked on Colleen.

"Commander, Commander," LB said, gently shaking her shoulder.

"Oh, um," Colleen sputtered. "LB, LB did you stop the roll?"

"Yes, Commander. We're stabilized now."

"Good, and what's the assessment of Hab?"

"RB is …"

"Right here," RB said, carrying the puppy container. "Hab took a direct hit and lost cabin pressure. The crops were frozen instantly."

"So, why do you have the puppy?" Colleen asked.

"I spotted a malfunction in the cryo chamber, so decided to initiate reanimation," RB said. "Fortunately, the inner container was small enough for me to carry."

LB had no interest in the puppy and could not understand why RB cared to save it. Colleen, however, was surprised to find herself pleased that it had been saved. Perhaps it was a symbol of hope, or maybe she just liked the idea of companionship. She didn't say, and the robots knew better than to ask.

"Alright," Colleen said, "I'll stay in Com while you two go back to Hab and see what can be done to salvage it. First, we need to find the hole and plug it. You know where the equipment is. Get moving. Sooner the better. Got it?"

"Roger," the robots said in unison before entering Hab through the airlock.

After checking Nellie's current heading, Colleen made course adjustments and then sent a very brief message to the Control Center so they'd know what had happened. She had few details to share, because she still knew very little about the problem. Colleen then checked all systems to assess the extent of the damage. Within minutes, she was able to confirm that the only damage was on Hab. The clear priority was to plug the hole if they could, and re-pressurize as soon as possible. She believed that the crops could be replaced later, but only by seeding and waiting weeks for regrowth. A major food source was now gone, at least temporarily. Colleen documented all of her findings for a report to the Control Center, letting them know that there would be an update after LB and RB completed their assessment of Hab. This was a huge mess, and Colleen knew she would need assistance from the Mission Team to determine the best option for moving forward.

The robots were designed for EVAs, so they had no difficulty working in Hab under freezing conditions with no cabin pressure. It took only a few minutes for them to locate the hole punched by the space debris. The hole wasn't too large, and they had what they needed to patch it. In fact, patching the hole may have been the easiest part of restoring Hab to a functioning state.

The tremendous suction created when the cabin lost pressure had relocated nearly every loose item in Hab, and many items were lost through the hole. Loose items that didn't make it through the hole during the rapid decompression were now floating freely inside the huge structure. There were multiple large dents around the hole, evidence that items had been sucked out at high speeds. Many larger items were floating near the hole, unable to fit through. Most of the garden plants were gone, having been snapped off and sucked through the hole after their instant freezing. The robots were initially puzzled by the huge chunks of ice that were found everywhere, but then realized they came from the crop irrigation tank which was cracked in half. The robots determined that the irrigation water had been released in two huge blocks of ice that were then battered around and broken up during decompression. Many of the larger chunks had apparently broken into pieces when slammed into the hole, leaving many smaller pieces floating about. After examining the situation, the robots carefully cleared away debris to create a working area around the hole for installing the patch. They worked quickly.

"Hole patched," RB said after putting on the final touches.

"Roger," LB said. "Pressurizing."

LB monitored the instrument panel to confirm that Hab was indeed being re-pressurized. All indications were good, so she increased the rate of air inflow from the pressurized storage containers. She adjusted the air temperature at the same time.

RB inspected the huge mechanism that rotated the cylinder to generate artificial gravity. Everything had shut off automatically when cabin pressure was lost. He saw no damage, so initiated rotation.

"RB, we need to save as much of the water as possible," LB said. Oddly enough, suction, the very thing that caused the loss of water, would be used to capture what remained from the irrigation tank.

The two robots worked for hours cleaning up the mess in Hab. They tested all systems and found little overall damage. The major problems seemed to be the loss of oxygen, food, and water, none of which affected them directly. They knew, however, that these were huge losses for Colleen, so gathered all of the information they could to create a comprehensive report for the Commander.

"At least Colleen is OK," Dave said as he and Jamie reviewed her message about the collision. "It appears that Carla's collision probability estimate was a little low."

"Right. We still don't know the full damage, however. The loss of oxygen may be a big problem, depending on how much was lost."

"She can make some through hydrolysis, and she has the equipment on board, right?"

"Yes, but that requires water, and we don't know if any water was lost. We'll have to wait and see on that."

"I just heard," Qadira said, entering Dave's office. "What do we know about damage?"

Jamie pointed to Colleen's message. Qadira raised all sorts of potential concerns, including whether the gravity cylinder would still be functional.

"Listen, Qadira," Jamie said, "we need to wait for the full assessment. There is no need to focus on all of the possible problems now. Let's get the report and deal with the actual problems, OK?"

"Yes, yes, of course," Qadira said. "You're right. I worry like it's my baby, because Colleen's survival could be at risk."

"We're all worried, Qadira," said Dave, "but she's alive and well now. So, let's go with that."

"We do need to think about whether Colleen can complete the mission, however," Jamie said. "She needs enough food, water, and oxygen to get to C and back. We have no idea what's available on the planet."

"Right," Dave said. "Let's pull up our records and determine what the levels of those supplies need to be to support a full mission. If supplies are short, we need to bring her home."

"We need to move fast, because she's less than three days away from the gravity assist," Carla said, entering the room.

"Thanks for coming, Carla," Jamie said. "You're right, and what we need from you is confirmation that Jamie has the correct set of commands for the assist to Earth. I know they were loaded on Nellie's computer before the launch, but we've learned a few more things about the planet since then, so we should update and adjust the approach parameters if necessary."

"OK, I'm on it," Carla said. "I'll work with the engineers and send an update to Colleen. It's good that it only takes 25 minutes for a message to arrive now."

"I'll work on the supplies problem," Jamie said, "but will need their full report before I can see where we stand."

"And Qadira," Dave said, "I need you to be available for any troubleshooting advice for Hab, OK?"

"Sure, I'll be here."

42

DAMAGE ASSESSMENT

Colleen reviewed the information the robots provided regarding Hab's condition. She was particularly concerned about the water loss.

"This is your best estimate of how much water we still have on board that's useable?" she asked LB.

"Yes, Commander," LB replied. "RB did his best to recapture as much as possible, but we lost nearly seventy percent of what was in the irrigation tank."

Colleen knew that such a large loss would put the mission in jeopardy. There were other water tanks that suffered no losses, but if she were to use some of that water to grow crops she'd have issues with her own needs, including maintaining cabin humidity.

"And what about the oxygen loss? How much is left?"

"We've replenished the atmosphere and now have a small reserve," LB said.

"What do you mean by small?"

"Our best estimate is five tons, Commander," RB said.

"We started with ten tons, right?" Colleen said.

"Yes, Commander," LB replied.

"And we can't produce any water or oxygen through electrolysis because we're short of both."

"Correct, Commander," LB said.

"And the crops all died."

"Yes, Commander."

"But you patched the hole," Colleen said with a chuckle.

"Yeeha!" RB exclaimed, wrongly sensing that this was a good time for fun.

"Control yourself, RB," LB commanded while attempting to swat him away.

Colleen simply laughed. "Leave him alone, LB. Maybe it is a good time for a laugh. What else can we do? It looks like we're doomed."

At that moment, the puppy stirred in its container next to RB's seat. RB reached over to check its status.

"It's fully awake now, Commander," RB said, reverting to more formal communication.

"Well, then let's free it from that cage," Colleen said.

RB opened the small hatch and pulled the puppy out. The young animal was obviously very happy, its urine floating in small, irregularly shaped yellow bubbles. Colleen laughed some more as the two robots struggled to capture and contain the runaway bubbles.

"Perhaps a doggie diaper would be a good idea," Colleen suggested. She quickly realized and was quite relieved to know that she had built-in puppy sitters, something she couldn't have imagined when she was younger. Her only task would be to enjoy the puppy. The robots would do everything else.

"Uh, yes, Commander," RB said before checking his data banks on "doggie diapers." "Yes, I seem to recall seeing some in Hab. I'll go get them," he said, handing the puppy over to LB.

"This will not be tolerated," LB said, attempting to reject the puppy.

"Oh, I think it will be good for you, LB," Colleen said. "Get the diapers, RB, while LB makes a new friend here." RB flashed a robot grin while LB struggled to hold on to the wriggling puppy. Colleen was enjoying the spectacle but, for some unknown reason, didn't want to hold the puppy herself.

After RB returned, the two robots struggled to put the diaper on the feisty puppy. Finally, after several minutes, the puppy's fluids were contained and RB set it into its cage just before a message arrived from the Control Center.

"It looks like they might be planning to send us back to Earth," RB said.

"They have to consider that option, RB," Colleen said. "They need the report on Hab, so please send that now and we'll see what they come back with."

"Commander," LB said, talking over the now-barking puppy, "Hab has been successfully restored for human habitation, and I believe that this four-legged creature has the same requirements, right?"

"Yes, LB, what are you saying?" Colleen asked, knowing exactly what she was saying.

"Well, Commander," LB began, the puppy barking even more loudly, "perhaps this creature would enjoy being in that much larger structure? It could run about, urinate wherever, and provide a little more room and comfort for those of us in Com."

"You don't like the puppy?" Colleen said, teasingly.

"I am not programmed to either like or dislike, Commander," LB replied. "I am simply making an observation based on the space requirements for us and the creature versus the space availability throughout Nellie."

"Wait a minute," Colleen said. "You remind me of someone I remember from when I was a kid. Are you, are you *Spock*?"

"No, Commander, I am LB."

Colleen chuckled, impressed by the clever job Frances Kelmar had done with the robots. Colleen hadn't recognized RB's Scotty earlier, but she could identify more with Spock, and the similarities to LB were now obvious to her.

"Never mind, LB. Yes, you can bring the puppy back to Hab."

Once again, LB had a hard time handling the puppy. The diaper, which had not been put on correctly, was nearly torn off as the puppy's wagging tail tried to free itself. While in the airlock, LB was given the opportunity to observe puppy pee from close-up range. As a result, LB sprung the puppy loose as soon as they entered Hab.

After things settled down again in Com, Colleen returned to the message from the Control Center. She had always known that there would be an option to return to Earth if things didn't go well, but she had dismissed it as a remote possibility. This was her only chance to reach C, and she was willing to have a one-way mission if that's what it would take. It made sense to her that humans should do all they could to contact intelligent alien life forms. She also knew, however, that the SSEA strictly prohibited sending humans on missions without an option to return home.

Colleen dutifully reviewed the commands for a gravity assist to Earth and made adjustments to the programming on Nellie based on the most recent Moriarty data. She would use Carla's work as an error check on her own.

43

TWO DAYS FROM MORIARTY

"They want us to go back to Earth," RB said as he viewed the Mission Team's detailed assessment with LB and Colleen.

"It is logical," LB said. "Food, water, and oxygen levels are all insufficient to keep the Commander going for the entire mission."

Colleen quietly gazed out of Com's observation window. Moriarty filled the dark sky, but Colleen could see only a dim outline of the planet. She then glanced at a monitor for an enhanced view of their target. Other monitors continued to register more debris passing by, but Colleen and the robots paid them little attention. They could do next to nothing to prevent additional collisions, so instead focused on how to respond if hit again.

"Wait a minute, Governor," RB said in a surprisingly good British accent. "You don't *need* to be active for the entire mission."

"What does that mean?" Colleen asked as she

turned her attention to RB.

"It means that you *can* complete the mission," RB said.

"No, no, I'm not getting into the cryo chamber," Colleen said, after catching on to RB's argument.

"Why not?" RB asked.

"It is not proven technology for this mission," Colleen replied.

"The puppy is doing well," RB said.

"The puppy *appears* to be doing well. That's the most we can say," Colleen said.

"That is true, Commander," LB added.

"This is the most important thing in your life, going to planet C, right?" RB asked.

"Yes, it is," Colleen replied.

"Then why would you let your fear of a little snooze time get in the way of getting there?" RB asked. LB tried to smack him, but RB deactivated her before she could.

"RB, what have you done?" Colleen hollered.

"Put her back on line, *now*."

"No, Colleen," RB said, addressing the Commander by her given name for the first time. "We need to talk without her interfering."

"This is outrageous," Colleen said. "I'm your Commander, and you need to do what I say."

"I'll do what you say, Commander, after you hear me out." RB lowered his voice a bit to calm the situation. "OK?"

"Make it quick."

"You are a very logical person," RB began. "a genius by human standards. Yet, you fail to recognize the value of your other half, the more human half of your being. For example, why didn't you hold the puppy? I believe you thought it to be a merely emotional activity that had no logical basis, no value. Ergo, you didn't do it despite wanting to."

Colleen squirmed in her seat, a sure sign that RB was getting to her. She wanted to argue with him, but couldn't think of what to say.

"You're also letting logic get in the way of doing what you really want to do on this mission. You've wanted to go to C ever since you were twelve years old, yet you won't do what it takes to get there because you fear the cryo chamber."

"I don't really fear the chamber. I just don't see sufficient evidence to show that it will work, so it's not a logical option for me."

"You actually *do* fear it in a way, Commander. You are afraid to step outside of your rational world and make a decision based solely on what you want, what you need. You fear using the cryo chamber because it doesn't make sense to you based on available information."

"I've never kept my desire to visit C a secret."

"True, but it has always been a linear process. You saw the potential for C to support life. You saw the evidence of intelligent life in the signals received from the planet. The next logical thing would be to go there and check it out. The risks of space flight were known, and it's logical to accept some risk in such a situation. Everything made sense, and there was no choice to be made between logic-based and emotion-based courses of action. Now, for the first time, you're confronted with what your mind construes as a clear choice between a rational path and a path based purely on desire. And you don't know what to do, do you?"

Colleen absorbed what RB was saying, and he could see that he was having an impact on her. She squirmed a bit more before saying, "How long will I need to be in the chamber?"

"That's my girl!" RB exclaimed, raising his hand for a high five that didn't come. Reeling himself in a bit, he said, "Control Center has provided us with data on how long supplies will last. I'll let you know what our options are shortly, Commander."

"Great," Colleen replied, "and reactivate LB. Make sure my cryo chamber is functioning properly. I want to know about the puppy, too. See if you can fix its cryo chamber and freeze it as well. We'll need to convince the Mission Team with some solid numbers."

Because he didn't want to be slapped immediately, RB erased the last few seconds of LB's memory before reactivating her. LB's immediate reaction was to announce another message from Earth.

"The frequency of signals from planet C has increased significantly, Commander," LB reported. "The cause is not known, but SUP and others seem to be encouraged by the news."

"Even more reason to head that way, Commander," RB added.

"Roger," Colleen said. "LB, we're going to C. Help RB with the cryo chambers."

"Roger, Commander." Despite being puzzled by the change of heart, LB dutifully marched off, asking no questions.

After an hour or so, RB reported that they had sent a message to Qadira regarding the puppy's cryo chamber. The robots were certain that they had made the repairs correctly, but protocol demanded a review from Earth. He also confirmed that Colleen's cryo chamber had not been damaged and appeared to be functioning properly.

"And what about the time I'll need in the cryo chamber?" Colleen asked.

"Well, Commander, our analysis shows a requirement of sixteen years each way," LB reported.

"Sixteen years?" Colleen hollered. "That's crazy. Are you sure?"

A Complicated Journey

"Yes, we've run the calculations several times," LB replied.

"But, if I may Commander," RB said, "please remember that this assumes a seventeen-year journey from Moriarty to C, using the seventy-percent assist path."

"That's right, RB," said Colleen. "That added five years each way. Let's argue for the full assist and then it'll be just eleven years each way. Eleven years ..."

"We do increase our risk of being hit again by space debris if we use that flightpath," RB cautioned.

"But only by a very small amount," LB said. "We've got better data now on the cloud, and the debris density doesn't change much between the flightpaths."

"It's settled then," Colleen said. "Let me have your numbers and I'll send a report to the Control Center."

44

ONE DAY FROM MORIARTY

"Can we let her do this?" Jamie asked.

"It does barely meet the safety criteria," Dave replied. "Seems a bit crazy to me, but what part of this mission hasn't been crazy?"

"I think we should let her continue on to C," Qadira said. "The risk doesn't change much."

"Agreed," Carla added.

"What about you?" Dave asked. "What do you think, Vera?"

Vera had been brought in to deliver an encouraging message to Colleen after the gravity assist, but the damage to Hab gave her a different purpose. She was then asked to convince Colleen that she needed to return to Earth, but the situation changed again with Colleen's message about continuing on to C.

"Colleen would have it no other way unless it was

illogical," Vera said. "And it appears that she has either grown beyond a pure logic-based existence, or the facts are aligned for a journey to C. Either way, I would grant her wish."

"OK, then," Dave said. "Jamie, please work with Vera to craft a message to Colleen about continuing on to C."

"Will you handle the press today?" Colleen asked.

"Sure," Dave replied.

45

DAY 934 – PRESS BRIEFING

"Good afternoon. I'm Dave Davids, SSEA Director. Dr. Bishop is busy working with Dr. Vera Daniels on a message to Commander Freeman. This message will grant Commander Freeman's request to continue on to planet C."

Dave then reviewed recent events that Jamie had described in briefings after the collision in the debris cloud. His goal was to keep the briefing as short as possible.

"Based on an updated risk analysis, we've determined that there is no meaningful increase in the danger of another collision if we increase from a seventy-percent path to a full-assist path. You should recall that we had considered getting a smaller boost from Moriarty to reduce the risk that Nellie would collide with debris in the cloud. That would have added five years to the mission, but we now see that there is no reason to reduce the gravity assist."

Dave answered a few questions about the risk analysis and what they had learned about the debris cloud. He then cast some images the robots had taken of damage in Hab.

"We just recently received these images of Hab after the collision. You can see the hole here. Some of the ice chunks can be seen here ... and here. Commander Freeman completed her assessment of the damage, including the loss of water, oxygen, and crops. We determined how long the existing supplies could support her within safety margins, and then sent that information to Nellie."

Casting a timeline, he said, "Dr. Freeman recommended, and we concurred, that she should go into hibernation using the cryo chamber for eleven years out and eleven years back to conserve resources sufficiently to enable continuation of the mission to C. As you can see here, she'll be awake for 200 days before entering the chamber. This will give her time to fully prepare Nellie for the long journey. There is still quite a bit of cleaning up to do after the collision, and the crew needs to do a significant amount of testing to confirm that all equipment is functioning properly. They'll also examine the Lander to make sure it wasn't damaged."

"What about the puppy?"

"The puppy will hibernate at the same time as Dr. Freeman."

"Why did you choose to go with 200 days awake now and 150 days awake before landing on C?"

"As I said, there is a lot to do to prepare Hab for the long journey. In addition, it ensures that Dr. Freeman will be awake when and after the asteroid hits Moriarty. She'll want to hear later about whether Moriarty's path has been altered by the collision. It'll take a few months for us to confirm the minute change in its path. Beyond that, it's simply her preference. The five months allotted before landing on C provides plenty of time to prepare for that event. That's all today. Thank you."

46

THE BIG ASSIST

Vera's message reached Nellie a few hours before the flightpath for the gravity assist had to be locked in. Colleen was both pleased and anxious. This was the first time in her life that she had sought something against her better judgment. Granted, it wasn't a radical choice, as the risk levels weren't substantially different if the cryo chamber worked as expected, but it was still a major event in her life. Receiving the message from Vera was a keen reminder of how far she'd come as a person.

"I look forward to chatting with you after the assist," Vera said at the end of her message. She hadn't forgotten.

Turning quickly to the matters at hand, Colleen ordered the robots to take their positions and ready the spacecraft for the gravity assist. RB brought the puppy back into Com despite LB's protestations. By now, the robots had learned how to put the diapers on correctly, so less pee filled the airspace. And the barking no longer bothered LB, because she had adjusted her hearing to block it out. Despite these improvements, bringing the animal into Com still made no sense to her.

Colleen transmitted a packet of current instrument readings and course headings to the Control Center for tracking purposes. In the event that communication was lost after the historic gravity assist, the Mission Team would need to be able to project the future location of Nellie to reconnect. They had never before communicated with a spacecraft traveling so fast and sought every advantage they could find.

"Accelerating rapidly, Commander," LB reported as Moriarty pulled harder and harder on the spacecraft. The slingshot effect was taking hold.

"Roger," Colleen replied. "Here we go."

RB was about to speak when LB suddenly slapped a sound barrier over his mouth. Not to be outdone, RB quickly cast a "Yeeha" message above their heads. Colleen chuckled as LB forcefully removed the barrier in defeat.

The trip around Moriarty was frightfully fast as

the spacecraft picked up speed. Even at such a rapid pace, the planet was so large that it took about five times as long to encircle than it would to encircle Jupiter. The monitors were constantly pinging with the near misses of space debris. At this speed, they all knew any collision would likely be fatal. The pinging simply became unsettling background noise.

"We're coming out on the other side, Commander," LB said.

"Roger," Colleen said. "Soon we'll be clear of the debris cloud."

Perhaps the puppy was a good luck charm, as none of the debris struck Nellie during the assist. RB glanced down at it many times during the wild ride. It seemed comfortable, quietly licking its paws. Even Colleen took a peek every now and then. LB completely ignored it.

"We're out of the debris cloud now, Commander," LB reported.

"And on to C," Colleen said, before adding "Yeeha!"

It took less than nineteen days for Nellie to pass

by the asteroid's position on its way to C. Moriarty and the asteroid would collide in about 123 more days, and by that time Nellie would be too far away for visual observation of the collision. In addition, the FFRs were on the wrong side of the asteroid to provide images, so the best options for tracking the event were satellites around Jupiter, several of which would be trained on Moriarty.

Colleen and the robots were making rapid progress restoring Hab to its original state, with the major exception being the hydroponic garden. With Colleen slated for two eleven-year sleeps, there was no compelling reason to repair and reseed the units. They essentially mothballed that area, but didn't dismantle anything given the outside chance that discoveries on C would change their situation.

Colleen developed a regimen that included workouts on the exercise equipment and some scientific readings. The robots tracked Nellie's path and tended to routine maintenance on the spacecraft. RB had assumed primary responsibility for taking care of the puppy, a job he thoroughly enjoyed. Communications with Earth had become routine, and the increasing distance led to much longer transmission times. It now took well over an hour for signals to travel one way.

47

DAY 1,058 – PRESS BRIEFING

"We have just confirmed that the asteroid has collided with Moriarty," Jamie said to the delight of the press corps. "Satellites near Jupiter have relayed images that show visible scars in Moriarty's atmosphere at the planned point of impact."

"Have you shared the news with Commander Freeman? Does she know she's a hero now?"

"Well, she is a hero, but she probably won't admit it," Jamie replied. "Yes, we have sent messages to her, but the first won't arrive for another hour or so. It takes nearly four hours now for a signal to reach Nellie."

"Would they have been able to observe the collision from Nellie?"

"No, Nellie was actually much farther away than we were here on Earth. At the time of collision, Nellie was over 3.6 billion kilometers away. That's just over 24.1 AUs, or three times the distance from Earth to Saturn. From that distance, the cameras on Nellie would be unable to register the collision in such dark space. Even if Nellie had taken images, they wouldn't be seeing them yet because it would take over three hours for the event to reach their cameras. For the record, Earth was about five AUs away at the time of the collision."

"How close were the satellites?"

"The satellites that provided our images were all about three AUs away from the collision. We used the images in conjunction with various satellite-based measurements to confirm that a collision occurred."

"Did it work? Has Moriarty's path been changed?"

"We won't be able to confirm whether the path of Moriarty was changed for a few more months. We hit our target as far as we can tell, but that's all we know at this point."

"Did the asteroid strike any debris in Moriarty's cloud?"

"We have no evidence that the asteroid was damaged before the collision."

48

MESSAGES FROM EARTH

"Message from the Control Center," LB reported. Colleen was on the treadmill at the time and RB was walking the puppy, both inside Hab where the artificial gravity had been fully restored after the collision near Moriarty. The puppy had grown some but would always be a small dog. Colleen and the robots stopped what they were doing to see the cast message.

"Yes!" Colleen said, pumping her fist in a rare display of emotion.

"We did it, Commander," RB hollered from the other side of Hab. He lifted the puppy and spun around.

"We'll have to wait and see if the asteroid did its job, RB, but at least we know we hit our target."

"There's more, Commander, but it's just for you," LB added.

"Roger, LB," Colleen said. "I'll take it in the

lounge."

With only one human on board, Qadira designed Hab to have a single private room that served both as a bedroom and lounge. Colleen slept and relaxed in her quarters during off hours. She toweled off after arriving, took a seat on the sofa, and cast the message. It was from Vera.

"Hello, Colleen. If you're receiving this message, it means that you succeeded in slamming the asteroid into Moriarty. Congratulations! I knew you would find a way to make the mission work, and you proved me right. I am very proud of you. And now it's off to planet C, the mission you've wanted to complete for so many years. Please heed my advice from our earlier communications. Take care of yourself physically, and try to find the joy in things. I've heard that you are doing well with the robots, particularly RB. That Frances Kelmar is truly a remarkable person. She seems to know how to add a special touch with her robots. Enjoy the journey, my friend."

Colleen later sent a reply to Vera, opening up about her crucial discussion with RB before the gravity assist. Colleen promised to enjoy herself more, and said she'd start by going out to play with the puppy for the first time.

After she left the lounge, Colleen called out, "Hey, puppy, come here!" RB was standing aside watching the puppy run around the garden. "Come here!"

The puppy had no idea what Colleen was hollering about. RB hadn't trained it at all. He simply changed its diapers, cleaned up its messes, fed it, and let it run around Hab.

"RB," Colleen called out. "What's the puppy's name?" She began walking toward RB.

"Name? Do these creatures have names, ma'am?"

"Yes, of course, all dogs and cats are named. You didn't know that?" said Colleen, now standing next to RB.

"Apparently, my programmer wasn't perfect it seems."

"Well, how do you get it to do what you want it to do if you can't call it by name?" she asked.

"I didn't think what I wanted would matter to the creature," RB replied.

Colleen laughed. "Oh boy, I need to report this to Jamie. You are absolutely clueless, aren't you?"

Colleen tracked down the puppy and scooped it up in her arms. It wriggled wildly while licking her face.

"It sure is a friendly puppy," she said.

"Yes, ma'am, but I do tire of cleaning my sensors after I hold her."

"Let's give, um, her a name," Colleen said after checking the puppy's gender. "I had a dog when I was a little kid. 'Tulip' was her name, and we called her 'Tuly'."

"Why didn't you use her name to call her?"

"That was her nickname, another version of her name that we liked better."

"Oh, yes, I see. These creatures can be complicated, can't they?"

"Actually, well, uh, never mind," Colleen said, not wanting to pursue that discussion point any further. "So, what should we call her?"

"I have no idea," RB replied. "You are the

Commander, so you should probably decide on the name."

"Yes, your program really is weak in this area, RB," Colleen said, smiling. "I don't want to use the same name, so how about 'Daffodil' or 'Daffy' for short?"

"As you say, ma'am. That shall be her name."

Colleen rummaged around the dog's cryo chamber and found a supply of dog toys that hadn't been used yet. She grabbed a toy stick and tossed it. Daffy immediately ran to fetch it, and a new friendship was born. Colleen's daily routine would now include play time with the dog.

49

DAY 1,119 – NEW PATHS

"Are we sure, Carla?" Dave asked. He had gathered the Mission Team to discuss the most recent findings on Moriarty's path.

"Yes, we're nearly certain," Carla replied. "Look here." She cast a simulation showing the current path of Moriarty. "All of the data points fall on the line with very small variation. We are 99 percent confident that the new path falls within the shaded area on either side of the line."

"And the red line, that's the warning line, right?" Dave asked.

"Exactly," Carla replied.

"And the shaded area comes close, but never touches it," Jamie added.

"Right," Carla said. "I think we accomplished our goal with the asteroid."

"In addition to Colleen, that makes you two

gentlemen heroes as well," Dave said to Lebron and Min.

Min was more relieved than anything because of the result. He took great pride in what he had accomplished, but was mostly glad to have the ordeal over.

Lebron, on the other hand, leapt with joy at the news. Never one to hold back his emotions and always a positive force, he slapped hands with everyone in the room before letting them know that there should be no doubt that he was not a hero. He was just another member of the team, plain and simple.

"Jamie, where's Vera?" Dave asked. "Wasn't she going to be here today?"

Jamie was looking down at her personal com device. She looked shaken, and soon tears began forming. She looked up at Dave. "She's gone."

Silence gripped the room for several minutes as Mission Team members shared hugs. Vera was a friend to some and mentor to others, but a giant in the field to all in the room. She had touched them all over the years with her grace and wisdom. Lebron and Qadira were relatively new friends, but both benefited from knowing her the past few years. Min, while failing to make it through her program, had found his way because of her. Dave had competed with her when they both were younger, but their mutual respect for each other was unparalleled. Carla was a dear friend and colleague. Jamie couldn't feel more indebted to her for all she had done over the years.

"Colleen needs to know," Dave said. "How do we tell her?"

"Vera will break the news herself," Jamie said, wiping away the tears. "She recorded a message weeks ago after a bout with pneumonia. She got sick just after the asteroid hit Moriarty. Somehow, she knew she was on her way out. She recorded the message on a good day before things went downhill for her."

"A professional to the end," Carla said. "And always thinking of others."

"Jamie, if you'll send word to Colleen about Moriarty, I'll take the press briefing for you," Dave said. "I think we should send Vera's message a few hours after the message about Moriarty so she at least gets to enjoy it a bit. Frances, is RB programmed for this sort of thing?"

"Yes, he is," Frances replied, "but he's a robot, so you never know how well it will be received."

A few hours later, there was celebration on Nellie as the news of Moriarty's change in direction was received. With little else to worry about during this part of the journey, Colleen gave everyone the day off. That really meant just her, because the robots had no understanding of the concept. Colleen enjoyed her break by playing with Daffy until the young dog was exhausted from chasing after toys.

After putting Daffy back in her cage, Colleen returned to the lounge and lay down. She felt as if a huge weight had been removed from her shoulders. Despite being wholly committed to the Moriarty mission, Colleen had always thought that she would be blamed for any failure because people knew that the trip to C had always been her real passion. Now that Moriarty had been moved from its path of destruction, there could be no blame and she could focus freely on C.

"Message for you, Commander," LB reported. "I'm relaying it to the lounge." At the same time, LB relayed a message from Frances Kelmar to RB, who was at his charging station.

Colleen sat up and cast the message. She could tell

from Vera's appearance that this wouldn't be a good message. As she listened, memories of her mentor raced through her head. Vera was the reason she was on her way to C. She was also the reason her outlook on things had moderated over the years. Because of Vera, she was no longer the bratty little twelve-year-old without any feelings. Colleen wept quietly before breaking into a full sob. She heard a gentle knock on the door.

"Not now," she said.

"But, Commander," RB replied from the other side of the door. "I know you're sad, and I want to help."

"Thank you, RB," Colleen replied, "but I just need some time alone."

"As you wish."

It was nearly a half hour before Colleen opened the door, and RB was standing there waiting for her. Hugging a robot seemed like an odd thing to do, but Colleen did it anyway. She had nobody else.

"Daffy is here to do what you want her to do," RB said.

Colleen smiled through the tears before saying, "Some day you'll catch on, RB."

After she recovered a bit, Colleen sent a message to the Mission Team. She first thanked them for how they handled Vera's death, especially the timing of the two messages. She then congratulated and thanked Min and Lebron for their work on the rockets and Barge. She added that she always knew Min had it in him, a comment that wasn't totally sincere, but pleased Min greatly. As a final note, she asked Frances Kelmar if she had ever owned a dog, a question that brought a smile to Jamie's face. Frances admitted that she hadn't, but wondered why it mattered. Jamie then cast the image Colleen sent showing Daffy wearing a diaper with her tail stuck inside instead of popped through the tail hole. A second image showed puppy urine floating throughout Com. Everyone but Frances was in stitches.

50

SLEEP

There were only sixteen days now before Colleen and Daffy would enter their cryo chambers. Colleen was beginning to dread being deactivated for so long. She knew that she wouldn't experience a thing during her deep freeze, waking up eleven years later believing she had just gone to sleep hours earlier. The worst part, she was told, was the period before entering the chamber. Colleen would certainly agree that it was a difficult time.

RB and LB were by now very familiar with the responsibilities they would have while Colleen was in the cryo chamber. They would check on the chamber several times each day, and continuous monitors would message them if there was any deviance from the optimal range of conditions in the chamber. They would also assume all of Colleen's duties, with guidance from the Mission Team. Colleen had no worries about any of these matters, as she had complete confidence in the robots. They had proven themselves to her many times over.

Jamie and Dave gave many pep talks in their daily messages, and Jamie had arranged for psychological counseling, testimonials from individuals who had been cryogenically preserved, and access to the engineers who built the chamber, so Colleen could ask them any questions she had. Colleen, however, didn't avail herself of those services, and simply enjoyed her communications with Jamie and Dave. The Commander assured them that she would be fine, and joked about how their differences in ages would appear to be even greater when she exited the chamber.

Finally, the day came when Colleen and Daffy would enter their cryo chambers. Colleen first helped the robots get Daffy ready. They medicated Daffy to calm her, and then induced a deep sleep after she was placed inside. Next, the chamber was turned on and suspended animation began nearly instantaneously.

Colleen was next. She took a long walk around Hab and peered out Nellie's windows to soak in everything she could before going into the long hibernation. She reviewed again with LB and RB their roles and responsibilities, thanking them for what they would do. She then sent a short message to Jamie before joining Daffy in deep slumber.

51

A NEW CONCERN

In their new routine, the robots kept Nellie on course and dutifully watched the cryo chambers to ensure that Colleen and Daffy would not be harmed during their eleven-year hibernation. Hab was nearly spotless after months of cleaning, and all instruments were performing as expected. The robots still hadn't worked on the garden because there was no plan to use it again, but they had ventured into Lander on occasion to ensure that everything was in good shape. The robot Janus would remain deactivated until after Colleen was reanimated prior to the landing on C.

On Earth, the Mission Team had little to do during the long journey to C. It had become a part-time job for most, with Jamie the only person fully dedicated to the mission. She communicated daily with LB and RB, but each day the transmission time increased by nearly two minutes. With 500 days to go before reaching the planet, it now took over five days for a message to be received.

Suddenly and unexpectedly, the mission was once again in jeopardy. Jamie received an update from Carla saying that SUP and others now believed they understood the nature of the signals from C.

"It's not good, Jamie," Carla said from her office at Hawthorn Tech.

"I've got Dave here with me now," Jamie said. "Tell us what you know."

"The research team in Spain has worked with SUP and teams in England and Japan to decipher the signals from C."

"OK," Dave said. "And?"

"And they believe there's a planet-wide war that's been waging for at least as long as we've been tracking the signals."

"What do you think?" Jamie asked. "Are they right?"

"That's not my area of expertise, but I know and trust the scientists on the team."

"So, are they using some sort of long-range laser weapons in their war?" Dave asked.

"That's the belief, yes," Carla said.

"Why such long-range weapons for a war on the planet? Isn't that just a waste of energy?" Jamie asked.

"Yeah, I thought C was supposed to have *intelligent* life," Dave added.

"You'd think so, Jamie," Carla replied, "but SUP also believes the war extends to at least one of the other two planets orbiting the brown dwarf."

"What's that based on?" Jamie asked.

"Not much, but, given the power of the bursts and the various trajectories they could measure, the team believes that there is some firing to and from the other planets," Carla said.

"OK, let's assume this is correct," Dave said. "We need a plan for Colleen. She's due for reanimation in just over a year. We can't let her get ambushed going in."

"She doesn't need to land on C," Jamie said. "She could loop around the brown dwarf and start back home. She'd get home faster than she would under the current plan, too, because she wouldn't need to launch from C and use gravity assists to pick up speed."

"Right," said Dave. "Let's work on some contingency plans and have them ready before she is awakened."

"Got it," Jamie said. "I'll bring on some more people and crank it out."

"And, Carla, please dig some more and find out all you can about the signals," Dave said. "Also, could you please find somebody to come here to brief us?"

"Sure," Carla said. "I've got good contacts, and I'll keep you posted."

"Has any of this leaked to others?" Dave asked.

"It's just a matter of time," Carla replied.

"Alright, Jamie, let's plan to talk with the press in the next few days so we can get ahead of the story," Dave said. "Carla, please let us know if we need to bump that up."

"Will do," Carla said.

"Colleen isn't going to like this," Jamie said.

"I know, and Nellie is not built for war," Dave added.

52

AWAKE

It was Day 5,111, and LB and RB were getting ready to reanimate Colleen. The procedure would take several hours. The two robots were prepared to administer medications for a variety of rare, but potentially dangerous, side effects, if needed. After reanimation, Colleen would need to rest for a few days while the robots ran a series of tests to ensure that she was capable of resuming her duties. Daffy would remain in her cryo chamber until the return trip to Earth.

"Are you ready, RB?" LB asked.

"Roger," RB said. "Let's bring the Captain back."

"Commander," LB said.

"I'm not your Commander," RB replied.

"Commander Freeman."

"She's not awake yet. Why are you calling to her?"

LB barely missed the back of RB's head, instead

smacking her hand into a wall and dislodging two of her fingers. RB helped her reassemble her hand after getting a promise from LB that she would behave. They then initiated the reanimation process. RB parked a hover chair nearby so they could transport Colleen to the lounge after she was removed from the chamber.

The two robots waited patiently beside the chamber, continually checking the instrument readings to ensure a safe recovery. Everything went smoothly, and Colleen began to show signs of life near the end of the procedure.

"It looks like she's almost ready to come out," RB said.

"That is what the instruments indicate," LB said.

"Confirmation of my observations is always most appreciated," RB said with a wink.

"And there we have it," LB said after a few more minutes. "It's time to open the chamber and help her out."

The two robots carefully checked Colleen's condition before giving her an assist from the chamber. The Commander appeared to have no symptoms or side effects, but was quite weak and a bit disoriented. They strapped her onto the hover chair and guided her to the lounge, where they lay her down on the bed with her head propped up.

"Greetings, Commander," LB said when Colleen appeared to be more alert.

Colleen tried to speak but could only grunt. The robots were not concerned, because they knew it was normal for the body to take some time before everything worked as before.

RB explained to Colleen that she would need to take it easy for a few days before she could resume command of the spacecraft. He also reviewed the procedures that would be followed to avoid misadventures while she recovered. It was, RB noted, a much more complex process for humans than for puppies. Colleen signaled her understanding.

There were now 150 days before the landing on C. Ideally, Colleen would have had plenty of time to prepare for the landing, but unbeknownst to her, there was now a war to consider. While Colleen slept, the Mission Team had been working diligently on ways to handle the situation. They had now just completed their assessment of options for routing Nellie around Finder 217, the brown dwarf. Despite there being another five billion kilometers between Nellie and 217, there were no viable options for redirecting the spacecraft to another celestial body for a gravity assist toward Earth, and there was insufficient power to change course without such a boost. Their preferred approach, therefore, would be to skirt around 217 at the greatest distance possible that would still provide the necessary boost to send Nellie home. They recommended jettisoning Lander before approaching C to streamline the spacecraft.

Carla found that the scientists evaluating the signals from C had not backed off at all about there being a war. In fact, the data lined up even better with their assessment over time. It was now a certainty that Colleen would face a dangerous situation if she attempted to land on C.

Jamie had directed the robots to not mention the war until a few days after Colleen was reanimated. They wanted to make sure that Colleen was reacclimated to the spacecraft and her role as Commander before she was confronted with the bad news. Besides, with their plan, Colleen wouldn't need to change course until a day or two before the encounter with 217.

53

CHANGE OF PLANS

"Message from the Control Center, Commander," LB said.

Colleen was now back to her normal self, and was running the spacecraft without a hitch. The robots had reported her rapid progress and confirmed to Jamie that she was once again perfectly capable of serving as Commander. Because it took five-and-a-half days for the message to arrive, Colleen had waited a dozen days to resume command. The spacecraft would now reach C in 138 days.

The robots sat near Colleen in Com as she viewed the message notifying her of the need to forego the landing on C. Colleen carefully reigned in her emotions as protection against any judgments by the robots about her fitness to continue as Commander. Getting too emotional at a time like this wouldn't help, especially after having been in the chamber for so long.

"Well, I see what they're saying, but we can't turn

back now."

"Commander," LB said, "I think you are well aware that you have received a command from the Control Center, and you are required to do what they say."

"Be sensible, ma'am," RB added. "You're likely to be killed if we try to land on C. There is a major war raging and Nellie has no protection against their powerful weapons."

"Look, we've come this far," Colleen began.

"And you saved Earth," RB interjected. "Humans don't need to settle on C now. There is no urgency to visit the planet."

"It would be most logical to return to Earth, Commander," LB said. "A lot has been learned on this mission, making it easier to plan a return trip under safer conditions."

"The first encounter with intelligent aliens should not be in wartime," RB said.

"I understand," Colleen said, realizing that the robots were right, "but this is a major disappointment. We're so close." Her voice fell off and she slumped in her seat. She held back her tears and motioned for the robots to leave her alone.

After several minutes, Colleen sent her reply to the Mission Team confirming that she would make the recommended course adjustments to loop around 217 for a return trip to Earth. She cautioned against jettisoning Lander, however, suggesting that it could be salvaged by leaving it in Mars orbit on her way back home. She also argued that it would provide additional protection from both space debris and alien weaponry. She further noted that Hab, not Lander, was the segment that made the spacecraft bulky, and it couldn't be jettisoned because it would be needed until Nellie reached Earth. Her arguments were well received by the Mission Team, and it was decided that Lander would remain with the spacecraft.

Nellie was defenseless against laser bursts or other weapons that might be used in the war on C. It had no weapons of any kind, nor any capabilities to maneuver in a battle mode. As such, there was little reason to prepare for battle, other than to consider options for signaling neutrality to avoid being fired upon if spotted before leaving the brown dwarf system. The Control Center provided Colleen with all of the data they could obtain from SUP and others so she could look for patterns that could provide some opportunities for communicating her peaceful purpose. They initially had no idea about what such patterns could be, but were hopeful that Colleen would be able to solve the riddle.

After spending over three weeks working with the SUP data, Colleen had found no patterns of interest. She concluded that her only hope of learning something about their communications would be to redirect her radio receiver from Earth toward C. That, however, would put her out of communication with Earth. Reestablishing communication with Earth later would not be too difficult, however, unless her flightpath changed unexpectedly.

"No, that's out of the question," Dave said after reviewing Colleen's request to redirect the receiver.

"I agree," Jamie said. "It completely violates protocol."

"What about using the backup receiver?" Qadira asked. She had been meeting with Dave and Jamie to discuss options for protecting Nellie against attacks, so was in the room when Colleen's message was received.

"Excellent idea," Dave said. "I hadn't considered that."

"It's on the Lander, right?" Jamie said.

"Yes," Qadira said. "It's not as sensitive, of course, but I believe it could work quite well within two AUs or less."

"That won't give her much time to collect and analyze the data," Jamie said. "That would put her at just under nine days away from C. Even with her capabilities, that's a very short time to learn a new language that may have no resemblance to anything we know here on Earth."

"It at least gives Colleen a chance," Dave said. "It could give her hope."

"I agree," Qadira said. "It's the best we can do under the circumstances."

Jamie reluctantly agreed and later sent a message that would reach Nellie more than five days later.

"I'd like to burn that protocol manual," Colleen lashed out after receiving the message.

LB was standing next to her and suggested that using the backup receiver had some potential. She volunteered to access Lander and set up the receiver so it could be operated from Com.

"OK, LB, let's give it a try," Colleen said, giving in to the suggestion. "It will make things a lot harder because of how close we need to be, but, you're right. It's better than nothing."

LB sent a message to RB to return from Hab where he was tending to Daffy in the cryo chamber. RB joined her as soon as possible, and the two robots entered Lander through the airlock and went to work.

Colleen sent a brief message back to Jamie. She was still upset about their decision, but saw no reason to fight back as arguing would only waste time. Colleen needed to focus on the task at hand. She also knew she needed as much help from the Mission Team as she could get. Colleen now had only 112 days to prepare for the approach and develop a plan for deciphering whatever language may be used in communications on C.

54

LANGUAGE 101

The two robots had the backup receiver operating within a few hours. They pointed it at C and listened in. After a few hours, they could detect no discernible transmissions, so moved on to other tasks until they were closer to C.

LB and Colleen reviewed the assist flight path recommended by the Mission Team and transmitted their concurrence. They entered the programming data to Nellie's computer and performed some preliminary testing to ensure that everything was ready to go.

Colleen then instructed the robots to test all equipment, including retro rockets, that would be required during the approach and gravity assist. Testing took several days, but in the end, it was determined that all systems were go. Colleen reported to Jamie that Nellie was ready to loop around 217. There would be only 95 days remaining before the assist when the reply was received from the Mission Team.

With the flight path now resolved, Colleen turned her attention to deciphering the methods of communication that might be used on C. The big assumption was that sound waves would be central to any communication methods used, but this was a very human-centric assumption. Colleen decided to have a session with RB in which they brainstormed on the range of ways intelligent beings might communicate using sound waves.

"Thank you, ma'am, for asking me to help with this," RB said. He had become used to Colleen just asking LB for help on technical matters. This assignment was a total surprise.

"We need to develop a plan for interpreting whatever radio signals we can receive from C," Colleen said. "We don't know how the aliens communicate, but assume they do because we believe they are at war. So, who would communicate with whom, what types of things might they communicate about, how might they use sound waves to do that, and what specific conversations might they have? These are the questions you and I need to address."

"And we need to develop computer programs to

evaluate the signals we collect against these considerations?"

"Exactly, RB. It's a lot to do in a very short time."

"I learned more than ten languages as a kid, yet I'm not really trained in linguistics. But I think you have some knowledge on the topic," Colleen said. "Is that right?"

"Yes, Commander," RB said, "but only a smidgen."

"Well, based on what you know, am I framing the questions right?"

"You've done well. Every language, of course, has a set of signs and symbols, the meaning of which may vary with social or cultural context. We need to try to determine the idea or meaning that the speaker has intended. This will require that we have a sense of references so we can understand if the individual is trying to indicate such concepts as big or small, few or many, safety or danger, love or hate, good or bad, and so forth."

"We need to simplify things and target our assessment to meet our needs, RB, rather than trying to develop a complete understanding of their communications," Colleen said.

"OK, then, what is our goal? What do we want to be able to do with their language?"

"We just want to tell them that we come in peace. We want them to not kill us," Colleen replied.

"Well, Klaatu," RB said, referring to the main character in an ancient film, *The Day the Earth Stood Still*, "we need to try to understand basic sentence structure and find those words."

"That makes sense. Let's get to it." And then she said, "Klaatu?" before adding, "Oh, never mind."

For the next six weeks, Colleen and RB asked Jamie for countless materials on linguistics, including seminars from the leading experts on the topic. Conversations with Earth were nearly impossible now with the long communication delays, so they sent sets of questions that the experts would answer in a follow-up message. Their understanding of linguistics grew rapidly.

Now armed with a solid understanding of linguistic methods, Colleen and RB developed an approach to gleaning sentence structure and identifying key words like "peace" from any radio signals they could collect from C. LB assisted by writing the computer programs for processing the captured signals. Everything was completed in 25 days, and Colleen sent the package to Earth for review and testing by linguistics experts. It now took about 11½ days for two-way communication with Earth, leaving the experts with less than a week for their review.

"That's right, Dave," Jamie said, "the linguists had only a few suggestions after testing the plan."

"Is there anything Colleen can't master?" Dave asked, before adding, "Well, anything not pertaining to people skills, I mean."

"Oh, she's even making progress there," Jamie said. "I've sent the comments to Colleen. She'll have three days to make some minor changes to her computer programs. They'll be ready to go with a little bit of time to spare."

"And then it gets crazy," Dave said.

"And we won't know a thing until it's over," Jamie added.

Colleen and the robots busily made the changes in their computer programs after receiving the message from Jamie. Colleen was quite pleased with how well they had done, but knew that expert reviews wouldn't matter if the plan didn't work in the end.

"Well, RB," Colleen said, "it looks like we're ready to go now. Another few days and we'll be collecting signals from C."

"Yes, ma'am," RB said. "We are prepared, but I think you should take the next day or two off so you're well rested."

"You may be right, RB. We've been working hard these past several weeks."

"You'll need to be sharp when the signals come in."

"Alright, I'll do what you say. You and LB can manage Nellie while I relax."

"Roger, Commander," RB said, satisfied that he was finally having the type of impact on Colleen for which he had been designed.

55

RACE AGAINST TIME

"Commander," LB said. "We have signals coming in."

"RB, you know what to do," Colleen said.

RB worked with LB to route all signals through the computer programs. Three-dimensional patterns detected in the signals were automatically updated and continuously displayed in the large working area they created in Hab. Colleen monitored the various holographic displays for patterns that could indicate sentence structure.

"There isn't much of interest yet, is there ma'am?" RB said.

"No, RB," Colleen replied. "The patterns I've seen are fleeting and too simple for the types of sentences that would be used by intelligent beings. It'll take awhile before we've collected enough signals for anything meaningful to develop. I just hope it doesn't take too long."

"Commander," LB said, "I have some audio per your request. The sounds they make are quite unique. They resemble none of the languages in our data banks."

Colleen listened to the squeals and grunts that seemed to constitute a spoken language. It was a relief to confirm that language on C was spoken, and that it fell within the auditory range of humans. The sounds made, however, were so different from those used in any language on Earth that she knew translation would be very difficult.

"Sounds like a hog farm," Colleen said to the amusement of RB.

"Hogs would have insufficient intelligence to generate these signals, Commander," LB said. Colleen and RB ignored the comment, returning their attention to the displays.

After three days, Colleen had not yet been able to isolate sentence structures. Without that breakthrough she knew that finding the right words to string together in a simple message of peace would be impossible. Because Earth communications were too slow at this point in their journey, she decided to have a brainstorming session with the robots to see if they could suggest changes in their approach that would yield better results.

"LB and RB," she messaged, "please join me in the lounge in five minutes. We need to think about other ways to solve this riddle."

"Roger, Commander," LB said from her position in Hab.

"Same here," RB said. He was in Com checking on the settings for the receiver. "Want me to bring Janus with me?" he asked flippantly.

LB chastised him, but Colleen saw some promise in the seemingly frivolous remark. "Yes, RB, bring her along. The more brains the better." The fun side of Frances Kelmar was again displayed in making Janus a female, an obvious play on words.

RB entered Lander through the airlock and activated Janus, a process that took several minutes. RB then ran some diagnostics to ensure that the third robot was functioning properly before releasing her from her chair. Satisfied that everything was fine, he led Janus to the lounge where LB and Colleen were already deliberating.

"Welcome, Janus," Colleen said. She rose from her

seat and shook the robot's hand.

"Thank you, Commander," Janus replied.

Colleen, LB, and RB reviewed for Janus what they had been doing with the signals, and described the results of their efforts. Janus listened intently, logging in her memory banks everything that had been said. They walked out to the work area and displayed for her the limited number of patterns they had discovered, none of which appeared to be meaningful. Colleen said they had only five days before reaching 217, with the chance of interactions with the aliens a day sooner.

"I see that you've all done amazing things in a short period of time, Commander" Janus said. "May I ask a few questions?"

Something about this robot already intrigued Colleen. She had observed Janus for only a few hours now, and had only very limited conversations with her, yet, there was something about this robot that appeared different, special even.

"Certainly," Colleen said. "That's why we're all here. We need to question ourselves and improve our methods."

"Well," Janus began, "have you considered the daily cycle of the aliens in your analysis?"

"Not really," Colleen said. "Why? Do you think the sentence structure will change between night and day?"

"It's not really that, Commander," Janus replied, "but my theory is that the war is fought mostly during the daylight hours as they used to be on Earth. There are many exceptions to that, of course, but, by and large, there is more war activity during the daylight hours."

"So?" LB asked. "We've clearly seen more activity during the daytime than during the nighttime."

"But, there's more, isn't there, Janus?" Colleen said.

"Yes, Commander," Janus said. "My theory is that the types of statements used at night will be different from those during the day because the noise of war will be filtered out."

"Meaning?" RB asked.

"Well, think of how fighters need to say a lot in very few words due to the rapid-fire nature of battle," Colleen said.

"Exactly, Commander," Janus said.

"So, with fewer signals of that type at night, the longer statements coming from more normal sources such as news broadcasts or entertainment will stand out more, right?" LB said.

"Yes, the battle communications will likely be very short, using a small set of standardized words," Janus said.

"Brilliant!" Colleen said. "RB and LB, work with Janus to update the code in our programs."

Within a couple of days, Colleen and the robots had detected several basic sentence structures based on the sound patterns. They still didn't know, however, what the squeals and grunts meant. They now had only about two days before reaching the outer planet, 217 a.

"Janus," Colleen said, "I'd like to talk with you in the lounge about the next steps."

Colleen had become very comfortable working with Janus. Her relationship with LB was computer-like, and that with RB was warm at times and ridiculous at others. Janus provided a balance that reminded her of something from her past that she couldn't quite pinpoint yet. Nonetheless, she believed working with Janus was now the best option for cracking the code of the alien language.

Janus joined Colleen in the lounge and they quickly began to share ideas about how to isolate words from the sentence structures they had identified. Again, Janus was invaluable in suggesting patterns to consider. Colleen applied her unique ability to recognize patterns and, between the two of them, they had identified several basic words in a matter of a few hours.

They then considered how statements might vary for different situations. News reports generally had consistent structures on Earth: for example, headlines, then national and international news, sports, and then weather. Janus suggested that aliens may have similar approaches, yet different groupings. Word selection would vary during these segments. Drama and comedy productions on Earth had their own structures, so Janus and Colleen also looked at the sentences with this in mind. They created new computer code to apply these new ideas and instructed LB and RB to run the signals through the new programs. They then waited for results.

56

COMMUNICATION

"Anything yet, LB?" Colleen asked, hoping to hear that they had discovered the words necessary to create a statement of peace. The three robots and Colleen were all gathered in Hab to monitor signals. The view from the front of Nellie was also cast so they could track the approaching planets.

"Nothing yet, Commander," LB reported.

They were now about to enter the region within 0.3 AU of the brown dwarf where the planets orbited. The planet 217 a would be encountered first, followed by 217 b and then 217 c, which was only 0.02 AU from Finder 217. Their approach was designed to be as far away from the planets as possible, but the planets' orbits were aligned in such a manner that they couldn't avoid C without traveling close to A and B. Colleen was understandably apprehensive about having to confront an alien spacecraft – if they existed – before breaking the language code.

"Commander," RB said, "the noise has increased more than ten-fold from yesterday. I believe the activity level is far greater than we imagined."

"A larger war than we thought?" Colleen asked.

"Roger," RB said.

Janus remained quiet, as was her normal practice. She observed much more than the other robots, speaking less frequently, but warranting greater attention from Colleen every time she did speak. Colleen was hoping she would have something to say about how to communicate with the aliens, the sooner the better.

Nellie was suddenly jolted by a blast of energy. All systems shut down briefly before resuming at full capacity. LB and RB scrambled to run diagnostics to assess the damage. Colleen clambered back to her feet after being tossed across Hab. Janus gave her a lending hand.

"What do we know, LB?" Colleen asked.

"All systems are fine, Commander," LB said. "It appears that we were hit by a laser pulse."

"Yes, Commander," RB said. "It was a laser pulse, but Nellie has suffered no permanent damage."

"Do we know the origin?" Colleen asked.

"No, Commander, but it was certainly not from any of the three planets," LB said.

"Indicating that they do have spacecraft," Janus said.

"And that we've been detected," Colleen added.

"RB, give me what you can on messages related to peace," Colleen ordered. "I know we don't have all of the words we need, but give me something close."

"Roger, Commander," RB said.

"I'll focus on finding the needed words, Commander, while you deal with the threat out there," Janus said. Colleen concurred, but was once again stricken by the familiarity in how Janus spoke to her.

"Commander," LB said, "it is unusual that the energy in the laser pulse that hit us is so much lower than others we have detected."

"Meaning?" Colleen asked.

"Perhaps they didn't try to hurt us," LB suggested.

"They were just contacting us?" Colleen said.

"Or 'feeling us out,' to borrow a phrase often used by humans," LB said.

"They simply jostled us," Colleen said. "But, is that a prelude to a stronger hit or an open door for communication?"

"One cannot say at this time," LB said.

"OK, then, our best approach appears to be to ignore it and focus on putting together a message for them," Colleen said. "RB, what have you got?"

"How about this, Commander?" RB asked. "With the words we know, we can say 'We stop today and be good.'"

"That's the best we can do?" Colleen said, frustrated.

Another jolt rocked the spacecraft, this time harder. Systems were back online again within seconds and subsequent diagnostics revealed no damage to Nellie. All agreed that there was no intent to harm them, at least not yet, but the pattern of increasing force of the hits was disturbing. How much longer could they survive?

57

DAY 5,261 – 217

As Nellie raced closer toward Finder 217, the laser pulses increased in frequency and potency, yet the spacecraft still was not disabled. The pattern clearly indicated that a response was needed to avoid destruction. Colleen was nearly in a panic, a highly unusual reaction for her. RB tried to calm her down, with little to show for his efforts. Janus stepped in.

"Commander," Janus said, "I believe I may have something now."

"What? What is it, Janus?" Colleen asked nearly hysterically.

"I think I have the words we need," Janus said.

"What are the words?" Colleen asked, impatiently as another pulse struck the spacecraft.

Colleen was tossed across the lounge, and Janus braced herself by charging her magnetic feet. Despite the frequent hits, Colleen hadn't taken any of the available precautions to prevent herself from being jostled, while the robots were all equipped to fasten themselves to the metallic floor in an instant. Colleen was bruised from head to toe, but wouldn't give in.

Janus cast the response just after systems came back online. The message sounded much like the squeals and grunts that Colleen heard in the very first signals they had captured, but the translation that showed indicated that the riddle had been solved.

"We come in peace," Colleen said. "Fantastic, Janus!"

In that moment, the pressure of the past few days seemed to be lifted from Colleen's shoulders and she returned to her normal, controlled self. She reached over to Janus and gave her a hug, and then she knew.

"You're modeled after Vera, aren't you?" she said, still holding Janus by her shoulders.

Janus merely smiled and asked "Will you be sending the message now, Commander?"

"Yeeha!" RB exclaimed after hearing that the

language code had been cracked, and the message was on its way.

LB transmitted the message on a wide range of wavelengths hoping that the alien spacecraft would receive the communication before sending another laser jolt their way. Nellie continued on its course toward the brown dwarf as its crew waited in silence for a response. Minutes passed with no additional laser pulses.

"Perhaps they have received the message, Commander," RB said.

"LB, anything yet?" Colleen asked.

"No, Commander," LB replied.

At that moment, all lights in Nellie were blackened and systems were shut down. Loud squeals could be heard from speakers throughout the spacecraft. Colleen writhed in pain and desperately covered her ears to shield herself from damage. Janus reacted instantly, neutralizing the sound waves surrounding the Commander.

Then there was silence. Dark silence.

"You will land your spacecraft," the message said.

Colleen smiled, temporarily losing all perspective on the situation. She was overcome with amazement and suddenly hopeful that her dreams for the mission would come true.

"Commander," LB said as the lights came back on, "we are no longer in control of Nellie."

"Don't worry, LB" Colleen said. "Everything will be fine."

To Be Continued

About the Author

Growing up not far from Cornell University, which Carl Sagan joined when Steve was in his early teens, Steve's fascination with the possibilities of space exploration began at an early age. He assembled model kits of the Mercury, Gemini, and Apollo spacecraft, and remembers watching scenes from the first moon landing on television. Steve spent many a frigid night observing the stars and planets at his home during high school, often having to quit because his telescope grease froze. Although an environmental chemist by training, he found time to enjoy an astronomy class in college, and has visited the Arecibo Observatory, the Jet Propulsion Laboratory, and the Kennedy Space Center. His most memorable experiences in the field, however, have been derived from tagging along with and following the research of his oldest daughter, Courtney, who is now an astrophysicist searching for inhabitable planets.

This book follows *Game Keepers*, which featured a magical world underground. *A Complicated Journey* turns its eye in the other direction, toward space, celebrating an entirely different kind of magic. Steve lives with his wife in Alexandria, Virginia, where they raised their two daughters and son.

CPSIA information can be obtained
at www.ICGtesting.com
Printed in the USA
FFHW012037110219
50509556-55761FF